Act II

Book Three of Tucker's Landing Series

Lina Rehal

Act II

Lina Rehal

Printed in the United States of America

Cover Design and formatting: coversbykaren.com

Version: 02.02.2024

ISBN-13: 978-0-9976150-6-7

ISBN-10: 0-9976150-6-7

Contact Lina Rehal

Email: rehalcute@aol.com

Websites: www.linarehal.com, www.thefuzzypinkmuse.com

Act II

Dedication

In memory of my husband, Dick Rehal, and the incredible journey we shared for three decades.

Special Thanks

Thank you to my family and friends for all your encouragement and support. If you critiqued a few chapters, shared my posts on Facebook, or assisted with my research by answering questions, you helped get me to the final draft.

I am especially grateful to my writing buddy, Mary. I couldn't have finished this book without all the emails, critiques, suggestions and coffee sessions.

Thanks to members of the Red Rock Rewriters for your comments, suggestions and critiques.

Thank you to all my friends on social media for the comments, likes and shares.

I would also like to thank anyone who takes the time to give this book a rating or review on Amazon. Those reviews mean so much to writers.

Thank you to all my readers.

Lina

Other Books by Lina Rehal

Early August

Chapter 1

Beth

Beth Piedmont sat in her dark gray SUV on the side of Beach Road and watched the steam escaping out from under its hood. The temperature outside was a stifling ninety-eight degrees. Tears welled in her eyes as beads of sweat formed on her forehead. Without air-conditioning, it wouldn't take long for the inside of the vehicle to catch up. The half empty bottle of water in the cupholder was already lukewarm. She fished a couple of tissues out of her bag, wiped her face and neck and thought about her desperate call to Triple A.

"I'm sorry ma'am. This heat wave is causing all sorts of problems. It'll be at least an hour before we can get someone out there. Are you in a safe place?"

"If you call sitting in a car on the side of the road in this heat with no air conditioner safe, then yes, I'm in a safe spot."

"We'll call you when the driver is ten minutes away."

"Thanks. I'll be here." said Beth.

I shouldn't have been so snippy with the woman. It's not her fault my brother's not home and not answering his cell phone. All I can do is wait for Triple A.

Wrapping her fingers around the leather steering wheel, she rested her head on her hands. Hot tears ran down her face and dropped onto her tan cargo shorts. Lifting her head, Beth swiped under her eyes with the back of one hand. She pulled down the visor and looked at herself in the mirror. "Oh. I look awful."

Beth plucked more tissues out of her purse. She wet them with the warm water and dabbed at the streaks of mascara on her pink cheeks.

She tried calling her brother again. "Dylan, where are you?" Beth said out loud. When he still didn't answer, she dropped the phone back into her purse. "I have to get out of this car before I pass out. Maybe someone I know will drive by. Great. Now I'm talking to myself like I'm stranded on a deserted island."

Beth opened the door, stepped out onto the road and stood a little away from the overheated vehicle. A dark blue Mercedes slowed down and pulled up in front of her car. The driver got out and walked toward her. His dark brown hair had touches of silvery gray at the temples. Over six feet tall, he was well tanned and impeccably dressed in Navy blue dockers, a white polo shirt, leather loafers and mirrored sunglasses. Beth was sure she didn't know him, yet there was something familiar about the man.

"You look like you could use some help. Is there anything I can do?"

Wishing she had kept her hair appointment yesterday, Beth pushed back a couple of limp curls that had fallen onto her forehead. "Thank you. It was nice of you to stop. I'm waiting for Triple A."

"Did they tell you how long it would be?"

She stammered. "Uh...um...about an hour."

He removed his sunglasses. "How long has it been since you called?"

His seductive brown eyes glinted in the sunlight. She wondered if he noticed that her tank top was soaked from sweat and clinging to her body. "About ten minutes."

He pulled a handkerchief out of his pants pocket and patted his forehead. "You can't stand out here for an hour."

"My brother lives down the street, but he's not home. I'll try him again in a few minutes."

He slid the handkerchief back into his pocket. "I live around the corner. You're welcome to wait at my house. I'll drive you back to the car when they call or to your brother's when he gets home."

As good as his offer sounded, Beth was leery of going anywhere with a strange man she met on the side of the road. "Thank you. I'll be okay."

"But you'll roast to death out here. "

He's probably right, she thought. *I feel like I'm melting.*

"At least come sit in my car while you wait. I left it running so it's nice and cool."

He put his sunglasses back on and smiled at her. "I have bottled water in a small cooler. Let me get you a water so you don't dehydrate."

How can I resist that gorgeous, sexy smile? He does have a point. I could really use a cold drink. But he didn't even tell me his name.

Beth smiled back at him. "By the way, my name is Beth Piedmont. I'd love a water."

His smile faded quickly. "I'm sorry. I should have introduced myself."

He extended his hand to her. "Ted Lamont. I'm new in Tucker's Landing. I really do live around the corner."

Ted Lamont? The famous playwright? No wonder he looks familiar. "You're Jonathan Blake's friend. You bought the house on Gray Goose Court from Fitzgerald Realty."

"Yes."

"Valerie Fitzgerald's a good friend of mine."

He laughed. "If I'd just told you that in the first place, we'd both be a lot cooler right now."

Just as he let go of her hand, Beth fell back against her car.

Ted reached for her. "Are you all right?"

She grabbed his arm. "I got a little woozy. I think I could use that water now."

He wrapped his arm around her waist. "And some cool air. I've got you. Only a few steps to my car."

"My purse. My phone's in it. They might call."

"I'll get it after we get you out of this heat."

She let him lead her to the car. *It's not bad enough I look like something the cat wouldn't bother to drag in, I have to go and practically faint in his arms.*

Ted opened the door on the passenger side of his Mercedes. Once Beth was in, he went around to the other side and got two bottles of water out of the cooler in the back seat. He reached in and handed one to Beth and put the other in the cupholder for himself.

"I'll get your purse. Be right back."

"Thank you," said Beth.

When he returned to the car, she was sitting with her head back and sliding the bottle from her face to her neck. He watched her for a few seconds with a whimsical look on his face.

"I think the idea is to drink it, not wear it."

"Ahhh," she moaned. "I know. It just feels so good."

Ted chuckled.

Beth twisted off the cap and took a long drink of the ice, cold water. Breathing a lot easier, she leaned back against the cool leather seat and stretched out her legs.

"Feeling better?" he asked.

"Much," she answered.

"You look a lot better. I thought I was going to lose you for a minute out there."

"You were right. I couldn't stand there for another hour or maybe more. I don't know what I would have done if you hadn't come along. You really are a life saver."

When her cell phone rang, Beth was almost disappointed to see AAA come across the screen.

"Ms. Piedmont, this is Darcy from Triple A. Are you still with the vehicle?"

"No. I'm in a neighbor's car with the air conditioner running at the moment. Is the tow truck on its way?"

"I'm afraid not. The driver's last call took longer than expected. It will be another hour before he can get there. I'm sorry."

"I see. Guess all I can do is wait. Thank you for the call."

"You're welcome. We'll let you know when he's on his way. Thanks for your patience."

Beth doubted she would have been so patient had it not been for Ted Lamont. *I hope I'm not keeping him from something.*

"Are they on their way?" he asked.

She turned and looked at him. "It will be another hour. I hate to see you using up your gas. Does that offer to wait at your place still stand?"

He smiled. "Give me your keys. I'll lock your car."

Chapter 2

Ted

Ted Lamont pulled into the driveway of his two-story home on Gray Goose Court. He glanced over at his passenger. He guessed she was in her mid-to-late forties. *I had to stop. What else could I do? With steam spewing from her radiator, the poor thing obviously needed help. I couldn't very well keep on going. Good thing I didn't. She nearly passed out from the heat. I sure as hell couldn't leave her standing there for an hour or more waiting for road service.*

She turned and smiled at him. Her deep brown almond shaped eyes were like two pools of dark chocolate. Even with streaks of mascara on her cheeks and sweat pouring off her, he could see she was pretty. Ted watched her raise the water bottle to her lips and drain out the last few drops. He wondered what it would be like to kiss those lips. *Better get inside before I need a cold shower.*

He shut the car off. "Well, here we are."

"I almost hate to get out, now that I'm finally able to breathe again."

"I promise you the house will be nice and cool."

He got out, walked to the other side of the car and opened the door. She grabbed her purse, swung her legs out and took the hand he offered. "I can't thank you enough. It was getting pretty hot out there."

Ted took the empty bottle from her with his other hand. "I've got a recycle bin in the house.

She followed him to the front door. "This is lovely," she said, as they stepped into the foyer.

6

"Thank you. I've been here a little over a month now. It's starting to feel like home."

She looked into the big, bright living room. "I know what you mean. I moved into my grandmother's house two weeks ago. I still have unpacked boxes."

He eyed her curiously but refrained from asking any questions. *So, she's new here too.* "Would you like another water or maybe a soda?"

"I'd love another water."

Ted rubbed his hands together and headed toward the kitchen. "Make yourself comfortable. I'll be right back."

"May I use your bathroom? I'd like to freshen up."

"Of course," he said. "Down the hall. On the left."

Ted went into the kitchen, got two bottles of water out of the fridge and returned to the living room. He took a seat on the sofa and thought about his unexpected houseguest. *I wonder why she moved in with her grandmother and who her brother is. She said he lives up the street. She didn't mention a husband and she's not wearing a wedding ring. Piedmont. Why does that ring a bell?*

He stood up when Beth walked into the room. She had combed the limp curls out of her thick brown hair and let it fall back over her shoulders. The fresh makeup and touch of pale pink lip gloss didn't go unnoticed either. Ted liked the transformation.

"You look great," was all he could say.

She laughed. "Thank you. I don't always have mascara running down my face. Don't worry. I didn't ruin your nice towels getting rid of the raccoon eyes."

He handed her one of the bottles. "It would have been well worth it. Come sit down. Can I get you something to eat?"

"Oh, no thank you. You've already done so much. But if you're hungry..."

"It's no trouble. Believe me. I had a small party here last night. There's a ton of leftovers. You'd be doing me a favor if you'd eat something. Do you like pasta salad?"

She was hesitant, but he was pretty sure she hadn't had lunch. "You sit right there. You gotta try this pasta thing."

Beth opened the bottle and sat back on the leather sectional sofa. In a few minutes, he returned carrying a tray with a bowl of pasta salad, salt, pepper and two rolls.

"Aren't you having any?" she asked.

"I'm not hungry. I was on my way home from having lunch with Jonathan when I spotted you. It's a good thing J B didn't have time for dessert."

She smiled and picked up her fork. "I'm glad of that. This does look delicious and you're right. I haven't eaten since this morning."

He figured as much. "The rolls are from Mia's. It's becoming my go to place for bread and pastry."

"Everyone loves her pastry. Her cakes are wonderful."

"I know. I had two of them last night and there's not one crumb left."

Beth lifted another forkful of pasta to her mouth. "This is fantastic."

"The wife of one of my guests knows I love it and made enough for two parties."

"Well, I'm glad of that too. So, how do you know Jonathan? Val told me you were friends back in Albany or something?"

Ted sat back and thought about his friendship with J B Blake, the well-known author. "Yes. Jonathan was a theater critic for a newspaper in Albany when we were both at the beginning of our careers. He reviewed my first play."

"Favorably, I take it."

He smiled. "Yes, but that's not why we became friends."

"I'm teasing."

"That happened when he started dating Nikki King, one of my leading ladies. He was around the theater a lot."

"I heard he was engaged to an actress once."

"Yeah. They were engaged for a while. It didn't work out. Anyway, I finally made it to Broadway and Jonathan became J B Blake, the novelist. We've remained good friends. He was the one who told me about this house."

She was finishing up her salad. "Why Tucker's Landing? What about your work?"

He shrugged his shoulders. "I write movies for television now. I can do that from almost anywhere."

"That's my point. Of all the fabulous cities, why this small town?"

Ted shifted in his seat. He leaned back and took a long drink. "After the divorce, my ex-wife moved to the North Shore to be near her family. Naturally, my daughter went with her."

Beth shook her head. "That must have been hard."

"I bought a condo in Boston to be closer to my daughter, but I still didn't get to see much of her. Meghan didn't like driving into town. I had to go there to see her. When Cynthia remarried, I went less often."

"Were you still in love with her?"

He shook his head. "No. But it was uncomfortable for me. My ex had a string of men she cheated on me with. I was pretty sure Marco had been one of them."

9

Beth didn't comment, but the look on her face told him she understood.

"Anyway…I had enough of living in a big city. I've always wanted to live on the ocean, and I've envied J B since the first time I visited him here. Meghan is twenty-five now and excited that I'm going to be close enough for her to visit. I'm looking forward to seeing more of my daughter."

He slapped his hands on his thighs. "That's my story. What about you? Obviously, you have family here."

"Yes. My grandmother and my brother."

She lowered her eyes for a few seconds and then looked back at him. "I live…that is, I lived, on the South Shore until my recent divorce. My mother wanted me to move back home, but my father and I…well…let's just say we often disagree. Besides, I wanted to get away from my life there."

He gave her a reassuring smile. "I get it, but why Tucker's Landing?"

"My mother grew up in this town. My brother and I spent a lot of time here when we were kids. It has happy memories for me."

"And your brother still lives here?"

"We never actually lived here. My grandparents did. He recently bought a house here. My grandmother has a big house out here on The Point. I'm moving in with her for the time being."

"Any kids?"

"A boy and a girl. They're grown and on their own."

"Do you work?"

She let out a big sigh. "I was an interior decorator, but my husband made me give it up when we started a family. We didn't need the money and he wanted me home with the children."

10

Recently divorced. Probably hard for her to talk about it. He changed the subject. "How do you know Valerie?"

"She's my brother's girlfriend."

Ted sat up straight. "Dylan Granger's your brother?"

"Do you know Dylan?"

"I met him when I first moved in. I almost didn't buy this house because I heard he was planning to build an office over his garage and block the ocean view. I see him and Valerie sometimes when I walk the beach."

She laughed. "That sounds like them."

Ted had another revelation. "Wait. You're a Granger. That means your grandmother is Josephine Rinaldi. The artist who lives in that sprawling estate on Three Point Bay."

"Don't tell me you know my grandmother. Although, she does know everyone in town."

"No, but I know of her. She's one talented lady. Does she still paint?"

"Yes. Mostly for her own pleasure now, though. She just celebrated her ninetieth birthday."

"J B told me her husband built that house."

"Yes, he did. When I get settled, maybe you'd like to come by for coffee. Gram loves company and she loves showing people the view of the Bay."

"I'd like that very much. I can't wait to tell J B about this."

She laughed. "What? That you met a Rinaldi?"

"No. That I picked up a hot woman on the side of the road."

When he saw she stopped laughing, he put his hand up. "Pun intended. Hot woman. Ninety-eight degrees."

He was glad to see her smile at him again. "I'd like to see the look on Jonathan's face when you tell him that one."

11

Ted picked up the tray and brought it into the kitchen. He came back with two more waters. "It's kind of funny because I was telling him how much I want to become part of the community, but I seem to be having a hard time meeting people."

"It's easier for me. I have family here and already know some of the people. I spent a lot of time here when I was a child. Did he have any suggestions? Other than driving around looking for hot women, that is."

He handed her a bottle and sat back down. "He said I should get involved in something."

"Like what?"

"He suggested I volunteer at the Tucker's Landing Little Theater. He thought I could help with auditions and casting for their next play."

She thought about it for a few seconds. "You know, that's not such a bad idea, for you."

"Why do you say it like that?"

She laughed. "Because my brother thought I should get involved with the theater too."

Ted wondered why Dylan would suggest that to her. "Oh, have you ever done any acting?"

"Mostly in college. I was involved in a community theater on the South Shore several years ago. But I'm sure he was thinking more along the lines of helping with stage designing."

"Oh? You did some acting in college?"

She shrugged her shoulders. "A little."

He raised his eyebrows. "Really? What kind of roles did you play?"

"Well, I did some singing and some acting."

"So, musicals?"

She waved her hand in the air. "You're a Broadway playwright. I know what you must think of college plays."

Ted smiled and looked straight into her eyes. "Beth, what do you think I did when I was in college?"

"You were in a college play?"

"What better way to learn? Now tell me, what was your favorite part?"

She looked away and then back at him. "I played Sandy in Grease in my senior year."

Ted gave her a thumbs up. "I'm impressed. I also think it's not such a bad idea for you either. Once you get settled, you should consider it."

Beth jumped when her phone rang. "Oh, maybe that's Triple A."

She pulled her phone out of her bag and answered it.

"Beth! Are you all right? Where are you? Why's your car on Beach Road with the hood up?"

"Calm down, Dylan. I'm fine. I'm at Ted Lamont's house."

She turned toward Ted. "It's Dylan."

"Ted Lamont. What are you doing there? What happened to your car? Never mind. I'll come get you."

"Dylan, slow down. I'm fine. The car overheated. Triple A was going to be over an hour. You weren't answering your phone. Ted happened to be driving by. He took me to his house to wait."

"You scared the hell out of me, you know that?"

"But you weren't at home and I couldn't reach you. How's that my fault?"

"It's not. I'm sorry. It's just that I thought something happened to you. I had a meeting in Boston and forgot my phone. I was coming home when I saw your car. I'll come get you."

Ted interrupted and reached for her phone. "Let me talk to him."

"Dylan, hi. It's Ted. Your sister's fine. Why not let her stay here until Triple A comes? We'll call you. I'll drive Beth to her car. You can meet us there and take her home. It'll probably be another half hour."

"Okay. Thanks, Ted. I'll be home waiting for your call."

Ted gave Beth back her phone and moved a little closer to her. "Now that that's settled, I want to hear all about your stage career."

Chapter 3

Beth

When Beth got home, Ann Potter, her grandmother's housekeeper and long-time companion, was waiting for her in the kitchen.

"Good Heavens, girl. Come in and sit. You look terrible."

"I know. Let me just wash my face."

Dropping her purse on a chair, Beth went straight to the sink, wet a paper towel with cold water and wiped her face and neck. "Ahhh. That's better."

Ann walked over to the refrigerator and took out a large glass pitcher. "Sit down, dear. I made this just for you."

Beth smiled. "Pink lemonade. My favorite."

The older woman placed the pitcher on the table and got two glasses out of the cabinet. "Dylan told me about what happened to your car when he called earlier to check on your grandmother. I made your room nice and cool. I thought you might like to take a nap before dinner."

Beth was touched by her thoughtfulness. "You've always taken such good care of us. But I promise not to cause extra work for you. I don't want to be a bother. I intend to help out around here."

Ann filled both glasses. "You're not a bother. I love having you here again and so does Josephine."

Beth was barely thirteen at the time, but she remembered when her grandparents hired a young woman to clean the big house on Three Point Bay. Ann wasn't much more than a child herself. At nineteen, she was a pretty, raven-haired girl with a wild streak, but she never missed a day's work and the Rinaldi's loved her, especially, Beth's grandmother.

"How are you and Gram doing with this heat?" asked Beth.

"We sat by the sliders in her studio for a while and enjoyed a beautiful ocean breeze coming in off the bay before she went in for her nap."

"I could have used that breeze earlier. Did you tell Gram what happened?"

"No, I didn't. No need for her to worry."

"Good."

Beth tossed the wet paper in the trash and took a seat at the table. "I don't know what we'd do without you, Annie. How long have you been here now? It has to be at least forty years."

Ann fluffed her short dark curls with one hand. "It's been over forty if you count from the beginning. I left for a few years after I got married and moved away."

Beth nodded. "I remember."

"When I came back to town, I was a single mother with two kids to support and no job. Your grandmother was busy with her career. She needed help with the house. Your grandfather hired me back full-time."

"Gram was so happy to have you back."

"When your grandfather passed on, Josephine asked me to move in and be her companion as well. I watched you and your brother grow up. I have fond memories of those times. You and Dylan are the brother and sister I never had."

"We feel the same way about you, Annie. I remember sharing secrets with you when I was a teenager."

Ann smiled. "We had so many."

"Yes, and you could always tell when I was leaving something out."

Both women laughed. Ann took a sip of her lemonade. "I could tell with Dylan too. I still can."

Beth stopped laughing. "What? You think he didn't tell the whole story?"

Ann eyed her curiously. "He said a neighbor who was passing by let you sit in his car to get out of the heat."

"Then he didn't tell you the neighbor was Ted Lamont and that he took me to his house and let me wait there until Triple A came?"

The older woman's soft brown eyes widened. "The playwright? Jonathan Blake's friend from New York?"

"That's the one."

"Funny, Dylan didn't mention his name, or that he took you to his home."

Beth took a long gulp of her lemonade. "He was playing the over-protective brother again."

Ann laughed. "I guess that explains why he called him your shining knight in a Mercedes."

"Honestly. He's so sweet and thoughtful most of the time. It infuriates me when he thinks I can't take care of myself."

"Don't be too hard on him, Beth. He loves you."

"I know. But still. It was embarrassing."

She finished her lemonade and yawned. "I think I could use a nap. I could definitely use a nice cool room after the day I've had."

"Not before you tell me the rest of it."

"What do you mean?"

"I want to hear about our new neighbor. What's he like? I know he's very good looking. I saw him at the supermarket one day. Was he a gracious host? What did you talk about all that time?"

Beth poured more lemonade into her glass and told Ann all the details of her encounter with Ted Lamont.

Ann was impressed. "It was certainly nice of him to stop. So many people these days just don't want to be bothered. Always in a hurry."

"Lucky for me, he isn't like that."

"He sounds like quite the gentleman."

"He is."

"You at least gave him your number, I hope."

When Beth didn't answer, Ann became suspicious. "What is it you're not telling me?"

"He wants to meet Gram. I told him I'll invite him for coffee. I hope that's okay."

Ann clapped her hands together. "Are you serious? Of course! Don't wait too long though. I'll bet there are plenty of single women in town who are trying to capture his attention."

"I'm sure there are, Annie. But I'm not looking for a relationship."

"I understand that, Beth. I'm only saying it wouldn't hurt to have dinner. It doesn't have to be a romantic dinner. Meet for drinks at the Black Rock. And give some serious thought to Dylan's idea about volunteering at the little theater."

Before Beth could answer, she was interrupted by the tap, tap, tap of her grandmother's cane on the tile in the hallway.

She got up, pulled out a chair and reached for Josephine. "Gram, just in time for some of Annie's pink lemonade."

"I can make it on my own. The cane is just to keep up my image."

Beth stifled a laugh. "How was your nap?"

"I'm feeling very refreshed, which is a lot more than I can say for you, my dear. You look dreadful. Are you all right?"

"I'm fine. My car broke down on Beach Road and I had to wait a while for Triple A, but Dylan came to my rescue. He brought me home after they towed my car."

"Nonsense. I know who rescued you."

Ann and Beth looked at each other in surprise. Josephine tapped her cane on the floor and sat down next to her granddaughter.

"Don't look at each other. Talk to me."

"You know it was Ted Lamont who helped me?" Beth asked.

"Of course."

"How did you find out?"

"Your brother told me. I may be ninety, but I'm not stupid. I had just gotten out of bed and heard a car in the driveway. When I looked out and saw Dylan dropping you off, I knew something must have happened to your car, so I called and asked him."

"But, Josephine," Ann stammered. "Dylan didn't even tell me about Mr. Lamont."

"I'm better at getting the truth out of him. He was afraid I'd find out on my own, and you both know I would have. He didn't want to face the consequences when I found out he lied to me."

Beth laughed and shook her head. "You're always a step ahead of us."

"I have to be."

Beth stood up and gave her grandmother a hug. "I think I'll go up and take a nice long shower and relax a little before dinner."

Josephine smiled at her. "Good idea. Oh, and you might want to call your hairdresser and reschedule that appointment you had for some time before Thursday."

Confused, Beth asked, "Why? What's so important about Thursday?"

"Your Mr. Lamont is coming for tea."

"What!" She looked at Ann and then back at her grandmother.

"Did you say Ted's coming here? How? Why? How did that happen?"

"Calm down, dear. I invited him a few moments ago. After I got off the phone with Dylan, I called to thank him for helping you. He told me how much he'd like to meet me and that you promised to have him over soon."

"Yes, Gram, I did, but I meant sometime in the future. Not Thursday."

"I know, but I'm not getting any younger and you do tend to procrastinate. I wanted to thank him for what he did, but I also have my own personal reasons for wanting to meet him."

Ann looked at Beth and shrugged her shoulders. "Look at it this way. The invitation came from Josephine. Less pressure for you."

Josephine looked up at her granddaughter. "Please don't be upset with me, dear. You know how I love having company."

Beth hugged her grandmother again. "I'm not upset with you. But you probably shouldn't let Dylan know about this."

"You go call your hairdresser and let me worry about my grandson."

Chapter 4

Beth

Beth sat in the swivel chair at Hair After anticipating the outcome of her new do. Looking in the large round mirror, she shuddered at the sight of herself in the black nylon cape. Carefully chosen tresses, wrapped in pieces of silver foil, covered her head. *I look like something out of a Sci-Fi movie. I hope Andre knows what he's doing. According to Val, he can perform miracles. He said just a few highlights.*

"Touching up the roots isn't enough. We need to liven up that mousey brown color with a few highlights. Your hair is thick and heavy. It's dragging you down. I'll add some layers and take it up a few inches."

She wanted something more manageable but was afraid he'd cut it too short. "Really? That much?"

"Yes. Trust me. It'll make the curls easier to manage, be more stylish and make you look younger."

She finally agreed to let him do what he was known for. "I'm all for looking younger. But, not too short."

As Beth absent mindedly flipped through the pages of a magazine, thoughts of Ted Lamont filled her head. *I can't believe Gram invited him to tea. I wish she had waited for me to do it. Of course, that probably never would have happened. She did say she had reasons of her own for wanting to meet him. I wonder what that's about.*

Beth stopped turning the pages. *I hope she's not playing matchmaker. I'm not interested in a relationship right now. I need to figure out what I'm going to do with my life. I have to stop dwelling on the past and concentrate on finding ways of reinventing myself. As for our sexy new neighbor, I'm*

21

sure he wouldn't give me a second look. I'm not even close to being in his league. But we do have some things in common. He seemed genuinely interested in my little bit of acting experience. It was nice to be able to talk to someone about the theater who didn't laugh at me or put me down about my college days. I wonder what he'd think if he knew I like to write.

When the timer buzzed, Andre hurried over and checked the color. "Let's get you to the sink and wash this out. Stop worrying. You're going to love your new look."

"I'm sure I will," Beth said to him. To herself, she thought, *I hope so.*

When he was done, Andre fluffed her hair out with his fingers, spritzed it with a little spray and placed his hands on the back of the chair. Their eyes met in the mirror. "Tell me you don't love it."

Beth turned her head from side to side. He was right. The new length, just above the shoulders, gave her a lift. She loved the blonde highlights.

"Valerie was right, Andre. You are a genius."

He smiled and shrugged his shoulders. "I try."

Beth bought the hairspray and mousse Andre suggested and left the shop feeling good about herself for the first time in months. *I can't wait to show Valerie. If I don't hurry, I'll be late for our lunch at the Portside Grill.* Once in the car, she pulled down the visor and took another look. She touched up her lipstick, buckled her seatbelt and headed for the restaurant to meet her friend.

Valerie Fitzgerald was the leading real estate broker in the area. She was also Dylan's girlfriend and had become Beth's closest friend over the past several months, especially since the divorce. Now that she was living in Tucker's Landing, it was nice to be able to meet for coffee and lunches.

When Beth got to the restaurant, Valerie was already seated. "Sorry I'm late. There was a lot of traffic. Hope you haven't been waiting long."

Valerie's mouth flew open when she turned and saw Beth. "You look gorgeous! Turn around. Let me see the back."

Beth laughed and spun around so Valerie could get a good look. "You were right. Andre is a miracle worker."

"There's nothing like a new hairstyle to perk a girl up."

Beth sat down. "You don't think he went overboard on the highlights?"

"Not at all. It's very flattering."

"Thank you. I can't wait to show Annie and Gram."

"I wonder what Ted Lamont will think when he shows up for tea tomorrow," said Valerie.

Beth picked up her menu and looked at her. "I really couldn't care less what he thinks."

Valerie put her menu down and took off her reading glasses. "Are you kidding me? The sexy new guy in town is coming to your house for tea. You have this fantastic new do and you're trying to tell me you don't care what he thinks. This is me you're talking to."

Beth hated that Valerie could see right through her. She put the menu down. "You're right. I do care. But it's only because I looked like such a fright when I first met him. No other reason."

Valerie put her glasses back on and picked up her menu. "Whatever you say."

"I was planning on a new hairstyle before I met Ted. You know that. You sent me to Andre."

"I know. I'm just saying there's nothing wrong with wanting to look good when you see him again. By the way, your nails look great too. I love the red."

"Honestly, Val, I'm not doing this for Ted Lamont's benefit, or any other man, for that matter. I'm doing it for me. Carl did a number on my self-esteem. I'm just trying to find myself again."

Valerie looked up at her and smiled. "Nothing wrong with that either. I know from first-hand experience and I'd say you're on the right path. You're a strong woman, Beth. You'll do just fine."

"I wish my brother could see that. He seems to forget I'm a grown woman. He was almost rude to Ted the other day and the man was only trying to help."

"I'm sorry he acted that way. I know what you mean. He is overly protective of you at times. I can see that. It's because he cares about you. It isn't that he doesn't like Ted. He just doesn't like him for you."

"I know, but that's not up to him. I'm aware of Ted's reputation with women. He's used to pretty young actresses. I'm sure he wouldn't be interested in me anyway. I think we should order."

"Yes, let's order. I'm getting hungry. But don't sell yourself short. Maybe the man is tired of dating starlets."

Beth laughed. "Yeah. A guy who looks like that is tired of having a beautiful, young woman on his arm when he goes to an upscale restaurant or the theater."

"All right. I give up. But, if he asks you out, I am going to say I told you so. Let's order. Then I want to talk to you about a business proposition."

Chapter 5

Ted

Ted walked up the front steps of the Rinaldi home and rang the bell. The scent from the roses he held in his arms made him wonder if he should have brought flowers for Beth too. *I don't want to convey the wrong message. Mrs. Rinaldi is the one who invited me. Besides, I don't even know if Beth will be here.*

When the door opened, a pretty, dark-haired woman, who appeared to be a little older than Ted, greeted him. "Hello Mr. Lamont. I'm Ann Potter, Mrs. Rinaldi's companion. Won't you come in?"

He stepped over the threshold and held out his hand. "It's a pleasure to meet you."

The woman's smile was warm and genuine. "Nice meeting you too. I'm glad you could join us for tea. Josephine is in the living room. Beth will be down shortly."

So, she will be joining us.

Ann led him into the foyer and closed the big oak door before turning toward him. "Are those for Josephine?"

He glanced down at the flowers. "I heard she likes roses."

"I'll let you give them to her and then I'll put them in some water."

He followed her into the large, living room. Josephine Rinaldi was sitting on one of the two ivory sofas. When Ann announced the arrival of her visitor, the elderly woman smoothed back her thick, snow-white hair and turned to greet him.

"Good afternoon, Mr. Lamont. Welcome to our home."

Ted walked toward her. She was impeccably dressed in black slacks, a long-sleeved, red silk blouse and a black and gray embroidered shawl with a ruby pin in white gold attached near her shoulder.

"Good afternoon, Mrs. Rinaldi. It's a pleasure to meet you."

"The pleasure is mine."

She nodded toward the flowers. "Are those for me?"

Ted looked down and then back at her. "Oh…yes, these are for you."

He placed the roses in her arms.

She lifted them toward her face, closed her eyes and breathed in the scent. "And such a pretty color. Dark pink is for showing gratitude you know."

"I do. It's my way of saying thank you for inviting me to your lovely home."

Josephine smiled. "It is I who should be thanking you for taking time out of your busy schedule to have tea with an old lady."

"Not too busy at all. I have one of your paintings of Three Point Bay. I've always wanted to meet the artist who painted it."

"Really? Beth didn't mention it."

"She doesn't know. It's hanging in my office. We got talking about the theater and I never thought of it."

"Well, you'll get to see the breathtaking view up close today. I'll show you my studio later and have Beth take you outside."

"I'd like that."

She gestured for him to sit. "Please, make yourself comfortable."

Ted sat on the opposite sofa.

Ann took the roses from her. "I'll put these in water and bring them into the dining room so we can enjoy them while we're having our tea?"

"Thank you, Ann. We'll move into the dining room when Beth comes down."

He looked around the large room. One wall was lined with shelves full of strategically placed antique bowls and figurines. Heavy gold drapes were open, revealing a lovely view of the perfectly landscaped yard through an enormous bow window.

"This is an impressive room. Did you do the decorating yourself?"

"Thank you. Yes, I did, but that was many years ago. It got a lot of use back then. We don't have parties and guests like we used to. I'm so happy you could join us today."

"I'm honored that you invited me, Mrs. Rinaldi."

"I'd like it if you would call me Josephine."

He smiled. "If you'll call me Ted."

"Well, Ted, now that we've dispensed with the formalities, I wonder what's keeping my granddaughter."

Suddenly, Beth appeared in the doorway. "I'm here, Gram."

Josephine turned toward her. "There you are. Come join us. Ann's getting the tea ready."

Ted stood as Beth entered the room. "Good afternoon, Beth. Nice to see you again."

"Good afternoon. I'm glad you could come."

She was wearing a sleeveless turquoise top and long, flowing white skirt. *Quite a transformation from the other day,* he thought, as she took a seat next to her grandmother.

"You look lovely."

"Thank you. I'm sorry I kept you waiting."

"That's quite all right. Your grandmother and I have been getting acquainted."

Beth looked directly at him. "I was on the phone with the storage company. They lost one of my boxes, but they found it and will drop it off tomorrow."

He nodded. "I understand completely. I know what a hassle moving can be."

"Except for that one box, I'm finally unpacked."

"Sounds like you've made some progress since the other day."

She laughed. "Seeing how organized you are inspired me."

Josephine chimed in. "Something else I should be thanking you for, Ted."

Just then, Ann came into the room. "Everything is ready."

"Thank you," said Josephine. "Shall we move to the dining room?"

Beth helped her up. "I'll get your cane for you."

Ted offered Josephine his arm. "May I escort you to tea?"

Her face lit up as she wrapped her arm around his. "Thank you. It's so nice to have a handsome gentleman around."

They all walked into the dining room. The long mahogany table was covered with a white linen tablecloth. A pot of hot water and a glass bowl filled with an assortment of teabags were in the center. Four places were set with matching napkins, small white plates, bone China cups and sparkling silverware. A crystal chandelier hung from the ceiling. Ted brought Josephine to her seat.

Ann picked out Josephine's favorite tea and fixed it for her before sitting down.

"Help yourself to blueberry muffins and scones," she said, as Ted poured for Beth. "We have butter or margarine and two kinds of jam."

"You set an elegant table, Ann. Did you bake all this?" Ted asked.

"Thank you. Just the muffins. The scones are from Mia's."

Beth noticed the roses in a crystal vase in the center of the buffet. "Where did the beautiful roses come from?"

"Ted brought them for me," said Josephine.

Beth looked over at him. "How did you know she loves roses?"

He smiled. "Valerie told me. I stopped by her office this morning to settle some paperwork."

"Valerie's a dear," said Josephine. "I'm happy for my grandson."

Beth reached for a muffin. "They do make a nice couple."

Josephine took a sip of tea, put the cup down and broke off a piece of her scone. "Beth, Ted has one of my paintings of the bay."

"Oh," said Beth. She looked toward him. "I didn't know that."

"I forgot to mention it the other day."

Josephine smiled at her granddaughter. "I told Ted you'd show him the view later, dear."

"Of course, Gram. I'd be happy to."

Ted wiped his mouth with a napkin. "Josephine, when we spoke on the phone, you mentioned that you had another reason for wanting to meet me."

Josephine placed her cup in the saucer and looked at Ann. "Would you please get it for me?"

Beth looked at Ted and shrugged her shoulders.

Ann stood up and walked over to the sideboard. She opened a drawer, took out a large manila envelope and brought it to the table.

"Thank you," said Josephine.

Holding the envelope, the elder woman turned toward Ted. "I have something I was hoping you wouldn't mind signing for me."

He was curious. "Something you want me to sign. I'm sure I won't mind, although I can't imagine what it could be."

She carefully pulled a booklet out of the envelope and placed it in front of him.

He stared at it for several seconds, then read the cover out loud. "*One Night in June* by Ted Lamont."

Ted looked up at Josephine. "It's a program book from one of my first plays."

"You needn't look so surprised. People from small towns go to the theater too, you know."

"That was close to thirty years ago. You've kept it all this time?"

"My late husband, Salvatore, was a musician in his younger days. He played the piano in hotels and restaurants in Boston when he was going to college to become an architect. That's where my grandchildren get their musical talents."

He looked at Beth.

"My brother plays the piano," she explained.

"He's quite good," continued Josephine. "But, like his grandfather, he wanted to be an architect. And I have no doubt Beth would have become an actress or a writer if her father hadn't been so set against her having a career."

Again, Ted turned toward Beth. "A writer?"

She looked away without answering him. "Gram, you're getting off topic. You were telling Ted about you and Grandpa going to the theater."

Not wanting to embarrass Beth, he dropped it. "Yes, Josephine. I'll gladly sign this for you, but I'd love to hear why you saved a program book all these years. Please go on."

"I'm sorry. I get distracted sometimes. My Salvatore loved the theater. We spent many exciting weekends in New York, staying in nice hotels, enjoying romantic dinners and going to the theater."

She paused for a moment and took a sip of her tea. "It was our anniversary. We couldn't get tickets to the play he wanted to see. It was opening night of your play in a small theater off Broadway. It looked like something we might both find interesting, so we took a chance and went."

Beth raised her hand. "I swear, I never heard this before."

Josephine smiled. "Well, it turned out to be a wonderful play. Salvatore said I should save the program book because someday Ted Lamont would be on Broadway. He was right. We got to see a few more of your plays and on Broadway."

Ted shook his head. "And you saved it all this time."

She picked up the envelope and emptied the rest of the contents on the table. "And our ticket stubs and the rose Sal gave me that night at dinner." She touched the exquisite ruby ring on her finger. "It was the night he gave me this ring."

Ted was overwhelmed. "What a beautiful story. I don't know what to say, except thank you for sharing it with me."

Beth handed him a pen. "Gram, did you ever imagine the man who wrote that play would be here signing the booklet you saved?"

Josephine looked down at the rose pressed in waxed paper. "Many times, dear. Many times."

Ted saw Beth brush a tear from the corner of her eye. "Beth, would you like to take a picture of your grandmother and me holding the book?"

"That's a great idea. Thank you," said Josephine.

After the photo, Josephine thanked Ted for signing her book. "I will put this with the other treasures in my memory box. When we finish our tea, as promised, I will show you my studio. Then, Beth will take you outside and show you Three Point Bay. Stay as long as you like and feel free to take pictures."

Chapter 6

Beth

Beth led the way through the back yard to an opening where part of the fence was missing.

"What happened here?" asked Ted.

"Part of it blew down in a recent storm. Annie's friend, Ed Farmer, will take care of it. He does odd jobs around here for my grandmother."

White puffy clouds billowed over the water. Temperatures were in the mid-eighties, much more comfortable than the day they met. A cool breeze was blowing in off the ocean.

"There's a spot over there where you can get some good shots of high tide if you like."

"What a spectacular view."

"It is. Gram never gets tired of it. She sits in that rocker and looks out at it every day. The house is built up high enough and the land slopes down, so she can see over the fence. Once in a while, Dylan brings her out here and sits with her so she can paint."

Ted walked beside her. "I can picture her out here sitting at an easel. I feel like I've been here before just from having one of her paintings. She really captured it."

"I've lost count of the ribbons she got for her paintings of Three Point Bay. Some with calm water. Many during a storm. A few with boats. Which do you have?"

"One with a gorgeous sky and waves smashing against the rocks. Almost looks like today."

Beth smiled. "I've always been amazed at how she could make them almost jump off the canvas."

He took out his phone and stopped to take a picture. "Do you have a favorite?" he asked.

"Any of her sunsets on the Bay. I have two of them. The sunsets here are the prettiest I've ever seen."

"I'll bet they're beautiful. Maybe you'll show me sometime."

Beth turned to look at him. He was staring at her.

She didn't understand the sudden flutter in the pit of her stomach. "The paintings or the sunset?"

He answered without taking his eyes off her. "Both."

"Maybe," she said, as she turned and started to walk again.

Suddenly, she stumbled and almost fell. Ted caught her arm.

"Are you okay?"

Beth grabbed his arm with her other hand and regained her balance. "I'm okay. The ground is very uneven here. I should have been watching where I was going."

"It's all right. I've got you."

"You always seem to be rescuing me."

He laughed. "You always seem to need rescuing."

He let go of her arm when they started walking again. She led him to a small white bench just before the rocky area. "This is where my grandparents liked to watch the sunsets. He put this bench here for that reason."

"Why don't we sit for a while? You can tell me how Three Point Bay got its name and why it's also known as Rinaldi Bay."

"Okay."

He sat next to her, took out his phone again and took more pictures. "This is beautiful."

She pointed toward the water. "You can see three places where the jagged rocks jut out forming what looks like three points. Two on one side and one on the other."

"Looks like a dangerous spot for any boats trying to come into the harbor."

"It is. Especially in fog or during high tide. You can't see them. Sea Captains were warned to watch out for the three points at the bay. That's how it got the name."

"Interesting."

"After my grandfather built the house, people around here started calling it Rinaldi's Bay, but it wasn't anything official."

Ted took a few more pictures, then looked at her. "Would you mind if I take a picture of you? You look so pretty and relaxed on that bench."

She immediately started fluffing her hair. "I'm not that photogenic."

"Oh, but you are. Let's take one and print it out for Josephine. Maybe she'll paint it."

Beth laughed at his persistence. "All right. But don't say I didn't warn you."

He stood and backed up just enough to get a good angle. "Okay. Don't look at me. Look out toward the ocean."

He took three shots and sat down to show her.

She was surprised at how good they came out. "Not bad, but please don't post it on Facebook or any social media."

"No, I wouldn't do that."

"Good."

"I've got another idea. Let's do something on this bench that your grandparents never did."

Beth moved away from him. "Excuse me!"

He shook his head and laughed. "I was talking about taking a selfie."

"Oh."

"I'm sorry. I didn't mean to embarrass you."

"You didn't."

He looked down at her hands that were folded across her knees. "Then why did your face turn as red as your lovely fingernails?"

She turned away from him. "I embarrassed myself."

"And now I've made you uncomfortable."

"I'm fine. Really."

He touched her hand. "Beth. Look at me."

Slowly, she turned toward him.

"I didn't mean to upset you. That remark about the selfie came out wrong and I'm sorry. But I won't apologize for paying you a compliment."

Now I've made him angry.

"In fact, I've been wanting to tell you how pretty you look all afternoon, but I didn't want to do it in front of Ann and Josephine."

No that's definitely not anger in his eyes. "I overreacted. It was kind of funny. Why don't we take that selfie now?"

Ted let go of her hand and moved in closer. He put one arm around Beth's shoulders and held the phone out facing the two of them. "I'll take a couple. Smile."

"Those came out nice," she said. "Let's try one standing with the view of the Atlantic behind us."

"For someone who didn't want her picture taken, you're getting into this."

She stood and put her back to the water. "You take good pictures. I may have to appoint you my personal photographer."

"I'm sure it has a lot to do with the subject matter."

He took a few more of the two of them and the bay before sitting back down.

They viewed them together. He deleted a couple of bad ones and sent her the rest.

Ted put his phone away and sat back against the bench. "I stopped by the little theater the other day and spoke to the director, Will Donaldson. They're looking for a new play. I think I might be able to help them out."

"Good timing."

"Yes. They would like to do something for Christmas. I told him I have a two act Christmas play from my early theater days that I would give them permission to use."

"Are you kidding? They'll love it."

"Have you given any thought to volunteering?"

She shrugged. "Some."

"What about auditioning?"

"Oh, I don't know about that."

"If I let you read the play, would you consider it?"

"I don't know, Ted. I haven't done much acting since college."

"Will you at least think about volunteering there? They could use your expertise on set designs. I think it would be good for you to be around a theater again. You obviously loved it once."

Beth became melancholy as she stared out at the bay. "I used to love a lot of things."

Ted reached over and gently turned her face toward him. "My guess is you still love the theater. Won't you at least give volunteering some thought?"

Knowing his guess was right, she looked back at him and smiled again. "I'll think about it."

"Good. It'll be fun for both of us."

He straightened and sat back against the bench. "Josephine mentioned that you like to write."

"That was a long time ago too. I even wrote a book once."

He raised an eyebrow. "Really. Ever try to publish it?"

She laughed. "No. It isn't any good. Or at least that's what my ex said."

"And he's an authority."

"No, but he was my husband."

"Which makes him the wrong person to judge."

She took in a deep breath and let it out. "You're probably right. He didn't want me to publish it."

He turned slightly toward her. "Would you let me read it?"

She lied. "I haven't even looked at it myself in years."

"Well, when you're ready and want an objective opinion, I'm here."

"It's nice of you to offer. I'll keep it in mind."

When she turned and faced him, Ted was staring at her. His expression was serious. The sensation of butterflies in her stomach returned. *I wonder what he's thinking.*

"I like what you've done to your hair."

She liked that he noticed. *Maybe Val was right. Maybe I did do it partly because of him.* "Thank you. By the way, it was sweet of you to bring my grandmother roses."

"Why do you change the subject when I pay you a compliment?" He sounded annoyed.

"Do I? I'm sorry."

"Look, I understand where you're at right now. I've been through a divorce too. Your ego can get a bit bruised, to say the least. I know mine did."

She couldn't imagine a handsome, successful man like him having a deflated ego. *Not with all the young actresses he goes out with.*

"You're an attractive woman, Beth. You're smart, talented, sexy, funny and you have a beautiful smile."

Now she could feel her face turning red. "Thank you," she said, almost believing it. "You're right about what divorce does to a person. You start to doubt yourself. I've only been on a few dates since. It's been a while since I've gotten that kind of attention from men. I'm just not used to it. Apparently, I don't handle it well."

Moving closer, Ted reached up and brushed a loose strand of hair behind her ear. "It's about time you get used to it again."

He leaned forward until their lips were almost touching. "I'll bet you haven't been kissed properly in a while either?"

"I have a feeling you're about to remedy that."

A shiver of excitement went through her as Ted closed the gap between them and covered her lips with his. She wrapped both arms around his neck as he pulled her against him. The mixture of salt air and the earthy scent of Patchouli almost made her lightheaded. With the sound of waves crashing over the rocks and gulls in the distance, Beth got lost in his long, gentle kiss.

Chapter 7

Ted

When Ted got home, he brought in the mail, thumbed through it quickly, tore up the junk and left the rest on the kitchen table. *Nothing that can't wait. I'll read it later.* He grabbed a beer out of the fridge, went upstairs to his deck that overlooked Gray Goose Court and sank into one of the lounge chairs. As he peered out at his own view of the Atlantic, images of Beth Piedmont and Three Point Bay filled his head.

He took out his cell phone and scrolled to the picture of her sitting on the white bench. Staring at the photo, Ted thought about how fantastic she looked in that outfit with her new hairdo and manicured nails. *She really is beautiful. Not the surface kind created by makeup artists either. Her beauty comes from inside and shines through. It's genuine.*

Beth is nothing like the women I usually date. She's not an actress looking for a part in one of my plays, or a young starlet wrangling for an invitation to a party where she can meet people important to her career. She doesn't want anything from me, or anyone else, for that matter.

Ted flipped to the photo of the two of them. *I can't deny I'm attracted to her. Judging by the way she kissed me back today, I think the feeling is mutual, even if she seemed confused by it after the fact.*

He put his phone on the table next to him, sat back and drank some of his beer. He tried to concentrate on work, but his mind kept going back to Beth and her reaction to what had happened between them.

After the kiss, she tried to back away, but he was still holding her. "Ted, I think we should probably get back. I wouldn't want my grandmother wondering what we're doing out here."

He loosened his hold on her but didn't let go. "Okay. But first tell me you'll have dinner with me tomorrow night."

She lowered her eyes and then looked back at him. "I'm not sure what just happened here and I'm not saying I didn't enjoy it, because I did. It's just that I'm in a difficult place right now. I'm vulnerable and confused. I can't get involved."

Ted smiled and kissed her on the forehead. "I understand. I'm sorry. I probably shouldn't have done that. Are you okay?"

"I'm fine. Thank you for understanding."

He dropped his arms and took her hands in his. "Beth, I don't have many friends in Tucker's Landing, and we seem to have a lot in common. I'd love to hear more about your experience in the theater and that book you're writing. Is there anything wrong with two friends having dinner together? Maybe I can persuade you to volunteer at the little theater."

She smiled and squeezed his hands. "No. Nothing at all. I'd love to have dinner with you. But I think we'd better get back to the house now."

"You're right. I don't want to get Josephine upset with me."

Yup, the feeling's mutual all right. But what am I going to do about it? I have to be careful. Beth's right, she's in a vulnerable position right now. Pursuing a romantic involvement would be a bad move on my part. Will I be able to keep things on a friendship level? Guess I'll find out tomorrow night.

Ted finished his beer, got up and went back downstairs. He opened his mail, made himself a sandwich, grabbed a soft drink and headed for the den to watch the news. After the news ended, he clicked off the TV and brought his plate back to the kitchen. When the house phone rang, he let it go to voicemail. *I'll get it later. I have a script to work on.*

Once in his office, Ted settled down at his desk. He worked with no interruptions for the next couple of hours. At nine-fifteen, he yawned, stretched his arms and closed his laptop. *That's enough for tonight.*

When Ted got in the kitchen, he saw the light flashing on the phone and remembered the earlier call. He pressed the button to retrieve his messages and grabbed a bottle of water out of the fridge.

"You have two messages."

The first was Jonathan.

"Hey, Ted. Just wondering how it went at Josephine's today. She's one special lady. Give me a call tomorrow. I'll be around this weekend. Maybe we can get together for a drink or dinner. Later, buddy."

He made a mental note to call him tomorrow.

Ted was about to take a drink of water when the next message began. He held the water bottle in mid-air when he heard the familiar sultry voice.

"Hi Ted. It's Diana. I know it's been a while. I'm back on the East Coast. Thought you might be lonely in that hick town I heard you moved to. I miss you, Teddy. Let's get together. Call me. Love you."

He screwed the cap on the bottle, put it back in the fridge and took out a beer. "Just what I need," Ted said out loud. He slammed the door shut. *I wonder what she's up to. Misses me, my ass. Loves me? Diana Lange never loved anyone but herself. Not even that Hollywood producer she married the last time we broke up.*

Ted looked at the clock over the table. *Almost nine-thirty. I'm not calling her back tonight.*

He went into the den, sat on the sofa with his beer in hand and thought about his on again, off again romance with actress, Diana Lange.

It began about eight and a half years ago, shortly after his divorce. Ted happened to be at the theater the day Diana auditioned for the part of Ava in his new play, It's Never Enough. At thirty-one, the voluptuous redhead was no longer a box-office draw. Hollywood producers wanted younger women to play their leading ladies. She decided to give up her waning movie career and return to the theater. Thanks to Ted, she got the part.

It was never much of a romance. It was always on when she needed me for something and off when she found greener pastures. We broke up at least four times in the five years we dated. The last being three years ago when she met and married some Hollywood producer who promised to get her back in the movies.

I'm tired of meaningless relationships with self-centered women who are only interested in what I can do for their careers.

He finished his beer and went upstairs to the master suite. Before closing the sliders, he stepped out onto the deck. It was a warm night with only a whisper of a breeze. Looking at the twinkling stars over the ocean reminded him of his afternoon with Beth. It made him think. *I'm fifty-six years old. It's about time I find a woman I can have a real relationship with.*

Chapter 8

Beth

Ever since she was a young girl, Beth loved the tranquility of early morning on the bay. When staying with her grandparents, she often sat by the water writing in her journal or contemplating the future. Today, she felt the need to sit on the little white bench down by the water and do some serious thinking. She filled a thermal mug with coffee, zipped her jacket and slipped out the back door.

Warmed by the hot liquid, Beth sat quietly and watched the morning fog lift. Sitting on the bench she shared with Ted Lamont, only hours ago, conjured up memories of yesterday. A shiver, that wasn't from the chill in the air, went through her when she thought about the way he kissed her. It made her wonder about the possibility of a relationship with the charming playwright.

Dylan says he's a player. I've never been able to play my whole life. Maybe it's about time I start.

She laughed at such a wild thought. *Who am I kidding? What would a man who's used to dating beautiful, exciting women, see in me other than friendship? Maybe Dylan's right. Maybe I am naïve. But Ted seems to understand where I'm at right now. He says he's okay with keeping our relationship just friends. Yet that kiss didn't feel the least bit friendly.*

Beth thought about the conversation she had with her grandmother after Ted left yesterday.

"I'll bet you're glad you went to the hairdresser now," said her grandmother.

"Gram, you know I didn't have my hair done to impress Ted Lamont."

"I know, dear. But, nonetheless, I saw the look on his face when you entered the room. He asked you out to dinner, didn't he?"

"Well, yes. But, just as friends. He doesn't know many people in town yet. Neither do I, for that matter."

Her grandmother nodded. "Your grandfather and I were best friends. That's important in a relationship, you know."

Beth sipped her coffee and smiled at the memory of her grandfather. *Gram married a good one. She can't possibly understand what I'm going through right now. The man she loved treated her like a queen. He encouraged her talent and would never have become involved with another woman.*

Beth wrapped her hands around the mug to keep them warm. She was annoyed at herself for allowing thoughts of her ex-husband to invade her solitude. She was devastated when he told her he wanted a divorce, but looking back on it now, she knew the marriage had been over a long time before that. *I should have divorced him the first time I caught him cheating.*

As the fog began to dissipate, patches of a clear blue sky peeped through, indicating another beautiful summer day. The weather reports promised temperatures in the mid-eighties with no humidity.

Beth took another long sip of her coffee and allowed her thoughts to drift back to yesterday and Ted. *He's easy to talk to and comfortable to be with. Comfortable enough for me to let him take my picture.*

She pulled her phone out and scrolled through the photos of the two of them. She'd been on a few dates since her divorce, but none of those men were as handsome or sophisticated as Ted. And none of them had kissed her the way he did. She looked out at the waves rolling in. *No one's ever kissed me like that. No one ever.*

Draining the last drop of coffee from the mug, Beth slipped her phone back in her pocket, got up and headed back to the house.

Ann was in the kitchen when Beth returned. "You're up early."

She hung her jacket on one of the hooks in the mud room. "I wanted to have my coffee out by the bay this morning."

Ann smiled, as she poured water over her teabag. "Even when you were a young girl, you liked being out there in the morning."

Beth rinsed out her mug and put it away. "I had some thinking to do."

"That's a good place to think and dream."

"Sounds like you spend some time out there yourself."

A faraway look passed briefly over the older woman's face. "Done a lot of thinking myself, over the years."

"And dreaming?"

Her smile returned. "That too. How 'bout some breakfast?"

"Thanks, but I need to get in the shower and get dressed. I'm meeting Valerie for coffee. She's offered me a part-time job helping her stage homes for open house events. We're going to talk over the details this morning. I'll get a muffin then."

Ann added milk to her tea and looked up at Beth. "That's wonderful! Does Josephine know?"

"No. Not yet. I just accepted her offer last night. I want to tell Gram myself later today. I have a few other errands to do and I want to stop by the little theater to see Will Donaldson about volunteering, I'll be back early. Ted's picking me up at six-thirty."

"Oh, that's right. You're having dinner with him tonight."

Ann lifted her teacup to her lips and smiled. "It seems Ted Lamont has inspired you to do more than finish your unpacking."

Beth put up one hand in protest and looked at Ann. "It has nothing to do with him."

"Uh, huh."

Beth knew she couldn't fool Ann. "Well, maybe the theater thing. But not the job."

Ann sipped her tea and put the cup down. "I'm happy about your job and that you're getting involved in something. It shows you are moving forward with your life. You have a good time tonight."

Beth gave Ann a hug. "Thanks, Annie. I've missed having you to talk to."

"Good. Because I want to hear all about your dinner."

Beth was smiling to herself as she walked out of the kitchen. *Well...maybe not about all of it.*

Chapter 9

Ted

Ted got up early Friday morning, had a quick cup of coffee and headed down the street to White Stone Beach. Since moving to Tucker's Landing, he had gotten into the habit of taking a walk along the water before the start of a workday. The ocean air and sound of the waves usually cleared his mind, but not today. Today, he couldn't get Beth out of his head.

She was afraid to get in my car. Not that I blame her. I hadn't even introduced myself. Later, at my house, she didn't push herself on me like some of the women I'd met in the supermarket. Beth treated me like a regular person. I can be myself around her. She may have seemed helpless that day on the side of the road, but underneath that guarded exterior, there's a strong, independent woman I'd like to get to know better.

After his walk, Ted showered, had breakfast, poured himself another cup of coffee and retreated to his office.

By noon, his stomach was growling. He sat back and looked up at the painting of Three Point Bay. *It was sweet of Josephine to save the program book from my play all these years. Such a gracious lady. I don't think she'd have a problem with her granddaughter going out with me. In fact, she'd probably encourage it. I wonder what Beth's book is about. I'd love to read it.*

Satisfied with the scene he'd been working on, Ted got up, grabbed his empty cup and headed to the kitchen. The light flashing on the house phone reminded him he had not returned Diana's call. *I'm not ready for that yet. I need lunch first. It's been three years since I've heard from her. Let her wait for a change. I wonder if she's still married to that producer.*

Ted thought about his ex-girlfriend while he made himself a sandwich. When Diana broke it off with him three years ago, Ted wasn't all that upset. He had been wanting out of the relationship for a while and had planned on ending it anyway. What really bothered him was being dumped and for a guy old enough to be her father. He knew not to take it personally. *That's how Diana is. The only thing the woman cares about is her career. She hasn't been in any movies lately. My guess is, she's no longer with him. The question is, what does Diana Lange want from me now?*

He sat down at the table and picked up his sandwich. *Doesn't matter. Whatever it is, she's not gonna get it this time. My life has been much less complicated without her and I intend to keep it that way.*

After lunch, Ted checked both his house and cell phones for messages. Thankfully, there were no more calls from Diana. *Good. I'll deal with her later.* There were two work related calls and one from Will Donaldson.

"Hi, Ted. Will Donaldson, from the Little Theater. I just finished reading *Mistletoe Madness*. I'm going to show it to the Board and recommend it. Having you oversee it and help with auditions would be a big help. Call me."

After taking care of business, Ted returned Will's call.

"I got your message. I'm glad you liked the play. "

"I loved it. The timing is great. We've been wanting to do a play with a holiday theme. This is perfect."

Ted was glad Will liked it. "That's great. I can make it more up to date, but I think it might be fine as is."

"I'm thinking the way it is makes it more nostalgic."

"I agree."

"An old friend stopped in to see me this morning. She used to do some acting in college and little theater on the south shore. She'd be perfect for the part of Lorna, but she might be a little too old."

Ted laughed. "Just how old is your friend?"

"Fifty-two maybe, but Beth could pass for early forties easily enough."

Ted thought about it. Lorna Hollingworth is a forty-one-year-old woman who has been secretly in love with her boss for the past six years. "It might be a stretch, but if your friend looks young enough...wait, did you say Beth?"

"Yes. Beth Granger."

"Do you mean Beth Piedmont?"

"Yes. Sorry. I knew her before she was married. She's recently divorced and is living here in Tucker's Landing. Do you know her?"

JB told me she's fifty-three, but he's right, she could pass for forty. He hesitated before answering. "Yes. As a matter of fact, I'm having dinner with her tonight."

"Oh...well then. I'm sure you know how talented she is."

"I've only known her a short time, but I know she did some acting in college."

"She can sing too. Voice like an angel. However, she doesn't want to. Volunteered to help with stage setting."

"So, you asked her to audition for the part of Lorna?"

"No. I wanted to run it by you first. But I did ask if she'd be interested in auditioning if there's a suitable role in our Christmas play. She said no, but maybe if you ask her..."

Ted wasn't sure that was a good idea. He didn't want to do anything that would jeopardize his relationship with

Beth, whatever it was. *What if I talk her in to auditioning and then she's not that good?* "Let me think about it. If the subject comes up tonight, I'll see what she says. First, let's find out if the Board approves the play."

"You're right. I'm meeting with them tonight. I should have an answer in a day or two."

"Good enough. Call me and we'll go from there."

Ted got a bottle of water and headed back to his office. Sitting at his computer, he re-read the script that was still on the screen. *Looks good. I may as well start the next scene.*

For the next couple of hours, Ted continued to work. When the words weren't coming to him, he removed his glasses and pinched the bridge of his nose between two fingers. *It's no use. I can't concentrate.*

He sat back in his chair. His thoughts immediately shifted to yesterday. Folding his arms across his chest, he looked up at the painting again. *And there's the reason why.*

Just how well did Will Donaldson know Beth? He didn't say they dated, only that he knew her before she was married. Was volunteering her only reason for stopping by the little theater? She couldn't have responded to my kiss like that, if she had feelings for Will. Or could she?

Ted took a deep breath and let it out. He shook his head and laughed. *Well, I'll be damned. I'm jealous.*

Chapter 10

Beth

Ted watched as Beth cut into her petite filet. "It looks just right," she said to their server.

"And yours, Sir?"

Cutting into his steak, Ted answered, "Perfect. Thank you."

"Enjoy your dinner," said the dark-haired waiter, as he turned and left them to their meal.

Beth unfolded the linen napkin and placed it over her lap. "This is so elegant."

"I wanted to take you out for a nice dinner."

She looked around the tastefully decorated dining room with its high ceilings, large windows and heavy drapery. "This is one of Boston's finest restaurants. The food and service are outstanding. It doesn't get much nicer than this."

"I'm glad you like it."

She couldn't help noticing how sexy he looked in a navy blue sport coat with the top two buttons of his white dress shirt undone. *I think "friends" may have just gone out the window.* She lifted her wine glass and smiled. "If you're trying to impress me, you've succeeded."

Holding his knife and fork, Ted leaned forward with both wrists against the table. "Of course, I'm trying to impress you. It's our first date."

Beth needed a minute to think about that statement. She touched the glass to her lips and took a slow sip of wine. *And so, it is.*

"I'm sorry, Beth. I probably shouldn't have called it a date. I wanted this to be a special night, since it's our first time out together."

She placed her glass back down and looked across the table at him. "There's no need to apologize. I'm having a wonderful time. You're a generous and thoughtful man. Any woman would be lucky to have a date with you."

Ted moved toward her a little and lowered his voice. "So, you wouldn't wear a killer dress like that to have dinner with a friend."

He's got me there. A black sheath with a lacy neckline makes a statement and he picked right up on it. "I guess I wanted to make an impression too."

"Well, you've made an indelible one on me. You look fantastic."

He picked up his glass. "I'd like to make a toast."

Beth raised her glass and waited.

"To friendship and wherever it may take us."

"To friendship," she echoed.

Conversation between them flowed easily for the rest of the meal. Beth was comfortable with him and felt like she'd known him for a long time.

"Tell me about your lunch with Valerie. You said something about a job offer, I believe."

"Oh, yes. She needs someone to help stage homes for open house events and thought I would be perfect for it. It's just part-time."

Ted nodded. "I'm sure, with your background, you'll do well at it."

"Thanks. I think I'll enjoy it."

"I know you will. You said you've been busy. What else have you been up to?"

She waited while the server filled their water glasses. "I stopped by the theater to see Will Donaldson. I volunteered to help with set designs and maybe auditions and casting if they need help with that."

Ted looked down at his plate. "I spoke to Will today. He told me you had gone to see him."

Beth detected something in his voice she couldn't quite put her finger on. "I went to volunteer."

"Not about auditioning?"

"No. Although, he did ask if I'd be interested in being in their Christmas play if they have one."

"He told me that too. Will also mentioned that you and he are old friends."

So that's it. He's wondering about Will and me. "Yes. I've known Will for years. We were once close friends. I lost touch with him after my marriage. We're going to catch up over lunch tomorrow. I'm sure he'll try to convince me to be in whatever play they come up with."

Ted took a drink of wine. "No. He wants me to do that."

"You?"

"I told him we were having dinner tonight."

"And he thought you might be able to talk me into it. They don't even have a play yet."

He held one hand up. "Technically, they don't. I gave him the one I told you about. He's going to present it to the Board tonight and let me know if they approve it. He thinks you'd be perfect for the lead."

"Ted, I haven't acted in years. I got involved in a little theater on the South Shore when my kids were in college, but I only played small roles. I really don't have an interest in doing it again. I'm not good enough."

"Will seems to think you are."

"His opinion could be a bit biased. And you've never seen me act or heard me sing."

"You'd have to audition like anyone else."

"What if you don't think I'm that good?"

"I'm a professional. There'd be no special treatment."

Beth wanted to change the subject. "Why don't we wait and see if the play is approved first?"

"How about going to my house for a nightcap? I could show it to you. You can take it home and read it if you want. If nothing else, it may give you some ideas for set designs."

She thought about Ted's offer while the waiter placed their coffee and dessert in front of them.

"I'll look at your play, but I can't make any promises. As long as that's understood, I'd love that nightcap."

"Fair enough. I won't push you. Now let's see what we can do about this White Chocolate Bread Pudding we ordered."

They picked up their spoons and dug in. "This is unbelievable," said Beth.

"Positively decadent." Ted laughed. "Maybe we should have ordered two."

Suddenly, a loud female voice interrupted their blissful dessert. "Well look who's here! Teddy, honey, I've been trying to reach you."

They both looked up. Ted dropped his spoon when he saw who was standing over them. "Diana. What are you doing here?"

"Having dinner with a friend. What else would I be doing here?"

Ted squirmed in his seat. "I meant in Boston."

"Well, if you returned your phone calls, you'd know. I told you I was on the East Coast."

He gritted his teeth. "I thought you meant New York."

"No, sweetie. Boston."

By this time, everyone in the dining room was staring at them. "Aren't you going to introduce me to your date, Teddy?"

Beth looked over at Ted. He faced her when he spoke. "I'm sorry, Beth. I didn't mean to be rude. Meet Diana Lange." He turned toward Diana. "Diana, this is Beth Piedmont."

The actress held out her hand. Beth knew it was a phony gesture, but she shook it anyway. "Miss Lange, it's so nice to meet you. I've seen most of your movies."

Diana glared at her. "It's always nice to meet a fan. Have you known Ted long?"

A waiter came over with an extra chair and offered her a seat. Ted stood. "That won't be necessary. Miss Lange can't stay. I'll escort her back to her table."

"Diana, Beth and I would like to finish our dessert and I'm sure your friend is getting lonesome."

"Of course, Teddy. I'll let you get back to your vanilla pudding. Sorry I interrupted. Nice to meet you Bess."

Beth knew the comment about the vanilla pudding was a dig at her and didn't appreciate it. "It's Beth. And it's White Chocolate Bread Pudding. Try it. It's to die for."

Ted took Diana by the elbow and turned her away from the table. "I'll be right back, Beth."

Once out of earshot, he lit into her. "What the hell do you think you're doing?"

Diana pulled away from him. "Why didn't you return my call?"

"I was working. I forgot. I would have called you tomorrow."

"Ted, I want to talk to you about something."

"We're done Diana."

"It's business, Teddy. That's all."

People were looking at them again. "All right. I'll call you tomorrow."

"You promise?"

"Yes. I promise. Now please get back to your table and let me finish my dessert."

"Oh yes...your bread pudding."

Ted turned and left her without saying good-bye. When he got back to his table, Beth was finishing her coffee.

He sat down. "It must be cold by now."

"The waiter brought a fresh cup. I told him to take the dessert away. I lost my appetite."

Ted covered her hand with his. "Beth, I'm so sorry. Believe me, I had no idea she'd be here."

"Of course not. You never returned her phone call."

He looked around. "I could use a drink. What do you say we go someplace quiet?"

Beth tried to smile. "Me too. How about that nightcap you promised me?"

Chapter 11

Ted

Beth was quiet on the ride back to Ted's house. He could only imagine what she was thinking after that awful scene at the restaurant. *Everything was going so well until Diana showed up. She deliberately tried to make it sound like there was still something going on with us. Damn her! I wish I hadn't agreed to call her tomorrow, but if I don't, she's liable to show up at my house. Can't let that happen.*

He reached over and covered Beth's hand with his. "You okay?"

"I'm fine. But a bit confused."

He kept his eyes on the road while he spoke. "I had no idea Diana would be there tonight. I didn't even know she was in Boston."

"I believe that."

He squeezed her hand. "I understand how upsetting it must have been for you. Tell me what you're confused about."

She shifted a little in her seat. "Ted...did Diana know you'd be there tonight?"

"No. I told no one. Not even you."

"She was that angry just because you didn't return her call?"

He rounded the corner onto Gray Goose Court. "Let's talk about this in the house."

"Because you need a drink to tell me about her?"

"Because I want to talk face to face with you so you can see I'm telling the truth. But I could use a drink to settle my nerves."

"So could I."

Once inside the house, Ted escorted her to the living room. "Make yourself comfortable. I'll get us that nightcap. Is brandy okay? I have wine if you prefer."

Beth sat down on the sofa. "Brandy's fine."

"Alexa, turn on some classical music," Ted commanded, as he walked toward a small bar in the corner of the room.

"All right," said a female voice. Beth laughed when soft music began to play. "I see you've done some updating."

"A little rewiring. She comes in handy when I'm carrying a snack into the den and I want to turn on a light or the TV."

When he came back with two snifters of brandy, Ted was glad to see she didn't seem angry. *Good. One angry woman a night is enough for any man.*

He handed her one of the glasses and sat down.

"Thank you," she said.

"Thank **you**," he repeated.

"For what?"

"For the way you handled a difficult situation."

Beth sat back against the big pillow. "How's that?"

"You kept your cool. Most women would have wanted to deck her."

"Oh, I wanted to."

Ted was surprised. "Yet you remained polite and civilized."

"Diana Lange isn't the only one who can act, Mr. Lamont."

Laughing, he touched his glass to hers. "You deserve an academy award."

Ted took a generous sip of his drink. He leaned back and watched Beth do the same.

She choked, patted her chest and shuddered.

"Go easy," he said. "This is strong stuff."

"I forgot how it burns on the way down."

She looked into her glass and then up at him. "Ted…you said we could talk about it once we were back at your house."

Oh, boy. Here it comes. "What is it that's bothering you, Beth?"

"It's really none of my business and you don't have to tell me…but…why didn't you call Diana back?"

He took another drink of brandy before answering. "The simple truth is, I forgot. It was late when I retrieved the message. I didn't want to deal with her then, so I decided to wait and call her today. I got busy and just plain forgot."

"But she was so angry with you."

"Diana is always angry with people who aren't at her beck and call."

"I couldn't believe the way she carried on in a public place. She's so beautiful and talented. It didn't fit her image."

Ted was a bit surprised himself. *Diana seldom lets the public see that side of her.* "Trust me. Her beauty is superficial."

"I know it's ridiculous, but she seemed jealous."

He put his drink on the coffee table and moved toward her. "That was an act. Diana's way of getting back at me for not calling."

Ted wanted to assure her Diana Lange was part of his past. "Look, I'm sorry she ruined our evening. She has no claim on me. We had a very complicated relationship, but I was never in love with her. We broke up three years ago when she married some Hollywood producer. I haven't seen or heard from her since, until that call yesterday."

Beth smiled. "She didn't ruin the whole night. I was having a wonderful time before that."

He smiled back at her. "So was I."

Ted looked into her beautiful brown eyes and knew he was treading on thin ice. *There's no way I can think of this woman as just a friend.*

She looked back at him and spoke in a playful tone. "Alexa. Does Ted want to kiss me?"

"Sorry. I don't know that," said the voice.

Taking the glass from her, he leaned forward. "I do."

Cupping her face in his hands, he felt the warmth of her skin. Her lips tasted of cognac. She slid her arms up around his neck. He pulled her into his arms. She played with the back of his hair and ran a fingernail across the top of his collar. It lit a fire in Ted he almost couldn't control. *Friends, my ass.* "You're driving me crazy. You know that, right?"

"I'm sorry," she whispered.

"Don't apologize." He nipped at her ear and kissed her neck. "Just keep doing it."

When Beth pulled away from him, Ted worried that he had gone too far. "Are you okay?"

She brushed her hair back with one hand. "Yes. I'm fine. But I don't think I should drink any more brandy."

He didn't think she'd had that much. "I'll just have the one. I still have to drive you home."

"Didn't you want to show me that play?"

He was glad she didn't want to go home yet. "Sure. I'll go get it. Can I bring you a soft drink or anything?"

"A diet something if you have it."

"Be right back."

"I'll just freshen up while you're doing that."

"Make yourself at home."

Beth went into the bathroom to touch-up her makeup and comb her hair. When she got back to the living room,

Ted was sitting on the sofa holding his brandy. The manuscript was on the coffee table.

"I brought you a diet Pepsi."

"Thanks."

She sat down beside him. "I take it that's your play."

"Yes. As I told you, it's a Christmas musical."

Beth picked it up and read the title out loud. "*Mistletoe Madness*".

"It's a two act play about an office romance."

She quietly thumbed through the pages.

He continued. "A secretary is secretly in love with her boss. She doesn't know he feels the same way. There's a strict company policy against employees dating. It all comes out when Lorna's offered a higher paying job for the Vice President of the company."

Beth closed the manuscript. "Act two. Jack kisses her under the mistletoe at an office Christmas party."

"Yes. He doesn't want to lose her…wait a minute. How did you know the ending if Will didn't tell you about the play?"

She held the script with both hands and looked at him. "Ted, I've seen this play."

"What? When?"

"When it opened on Broadway."

"You were there?"

"I went to New York on a girls' weekend with two of my friends. It was just after Thanksgiving. We had the best time."

Ted put his drink down. He sat back and looked at her curiously. "What made you pick my play?"

"We wanted to see a Christmas play. Our waiter at the restaurant where we had dinner suggested it. He said a new play by Ted Lamont was opening that night. He helped us get tickets."

"You knew who I was?"

"No, not then."

He smiled. "You're not going to tell me you kept the playbill, are you?"

She laughed. "No. But I'll never forget it."

"So, does that mean you liked it?"

Beth held the script against her chest. "I was singing the songs for weeks. It drove Carl crazy."

He noticed that was the first time she'd mentioned her ex by name. "Beth...would you consider auditioning now?"

"Me? Play the part of Lorna Hollingsworth?"

"Why not? You already know the part."

Beth shook her head and looked away. "I don't think so."

Ted was almost certain he could convince her. "I'll bet you still know all the songs too."

She placed the script back on the table and faced him again. "I've been away from it too long, Ted."

He sat forward again and moved to the edge of the sofa. "Beth, you love the theater. Please. Just take it with you and think about it. Talk it over with Will when you have lunch with him. Only, please don't wear that dress."

She reached for her diet soda. "I think we already determined it's not a dress for friends."

"I was teasing...sort of. I realize I have no right to tell you what to wear."

"I'm glad you like the dress."

He picked up his drink and sat back against the pillows. His expression turned serious. "Can I ask you something?"

"Of course."

Ted had a feeling her reasons for not wanting to audition had to do with the ex. *Maybe if I can get her to talk about it, she'll change her mind.* "You mentioned being involved in a little theater when your kids were in college."

"I was looking for something to do. I didn't do it for long."

"Why did you stop?"

She lowered her eyes. "Same reason I gave up my job as an interior decorator. Carl."

"Your ex didn't want you doing it?"

"He didn't seem to mind at first. I only played a couple of bit parts, it made me feel useful and alive again. I liked being part of something."

"And he made you give it up."

"I was an understudy. On the third night, the leading lady got sick. I had to take her place. Somehow, I talked him into going that night to see me. He couldn't handle the attention I got. Told me later I wasn't that good."

Ted shook his head. *I was right. The jerk sabotaged her self-esteem.* "So, he forced you to quit."

"When the local paper did an article about me, he decided I was away from home too much. He said they were just being nice to me because he was on the board of the newspaper. I quit and vowed to never act again."

Ted wanted to know more about her marriage so he could better understand where she was coming from. "You must have loved him a lot to give up so much of yourself."

"I did in the beginning. He was handsome, smart, successful. But success changed him. I learned to look the other way a lot."

"He was unfaithful?"

"Probably more times than I knew about."

Ted could understand that. "Why did you stay with him?"

Beth shrugged her shoulders. "Mostly for the kids."

She took a long drink of her soda and looked away. "I was also afraid of being divorced and alone. Carl was a lousy husband, but he was a good provider. He always had to have the best of everything. A beautiful home, nice clothes, fancy cars. We ate in the best restaurants and went on great vacations. Even had a summer home."

"Were you happy living like that?"

She turned and looked at him again. "You mean in my fantasy world? Not since the first time he cheated on me. Or at least the first time I found out."

"I've been there. It's rough."

She put her soda down and picked up the brandy. "I think I might have a little more of this."

He leaned forward. "If you'd rather not talk about it, it's okay."

She took a small taste of the brandy, without choking this time. "No. I want to tell you."

Ted sat back and let her continue.

"The first time I suspected he was cheating, I ignored it. I thought he'd get tired of her. Eventually, he did. Then a year later, the signs were all there again. I confronted him with my suspicions. He denied it at first, but finally admitted the truth and promised it would never happen again."

It was all so familiar to Ted. "But it did, of course."

"Several times. Then about eight years ago, he had an affair with a married woman. It happened while we were staying at our cottage on Cape Cod."

Something clicked in Ted's brain. He shifted nervously in his seat. "You had a place on the Cape?"

"Yes. West Yarmouth."

It has to be just a coincidence, he thought.

"The woman had been spending the summer with family in Hyannis. I ignored the gossip that was going around town until a neighbor told me she had seen Carl having dinner with a woman. I asked him about it."

"What did he say?"

She laughed. "He said she was a client."

"A client?"

"I'm sorry. I guess I never told you what Carl does. He manufactures custom draperies and upholstery for hotels, restaurants, resorts and expensive homes."

He swallowed the last drop of his brandy. "No...you hadn't mentioned it."

"That's how we met. I was decorating a home and got the drapes from him. It was before he built Imperial Drapes into the big company it is now."

A knot formed in Ted's stomach. "How did you find out the woman wasn't a client?"

"I saw his car in front of a motel in Falmouth on my way home from visiting a friend. This time I flat out accused him of having an affair. He denied it until I threatened to leave him."

"But...he didn't tell you the woman's name?"

"No. And I didn't ask. He swore it was over. Supposedly, her husband found out and she went home to New Jersey or New York. I stayed with him, but the marriage was over for me long before he asked for a divorce."

Ted's jaw tightened, as he fit the pieces together. Unable to look at Beth, he put the empty snifter down, got up and walked over to the window. *If only she'd mentioned his first name or what he does for a living sooner.*

Beth turned. "Are you okay? Did I say something I shouldn't have?"

Ted regained his composure and sat down beside her. "No. Not at all. Just remembering some unpleasant memories of my own."

I need to think about how to handle this. I can't just blurt out that the married woman her ex was with eight years ago was my wife. She'd wonder why I didn't say anything sooner. She'll never believe I hadn't realized it until just now. Boy that Carl Piedmont is some piece of work.

She put her almost empty glass on the table. He took both her hands in his. "I understand why you don't want to act again. Really, I do. But you love the theater, Beth. Don't let him take that away from you. Take the script home. Think about it. Talk to Will. You can read some of it for me in private. I'll help you with it."

"But you've never seen me perform. What if you don't think I'm right for the part of Lorna?"

"Then I'll re-write it to suit you. If you could play Sandy, you can do Lorna."

She gave him a faint smile. "What am I going to do with you?"

"Come 'ere and I'll show you."

He pulled her into his arms. "Alexa, turn down the lights."

Chapter 12

Beth

It was close to midnight when Ted drove Beth home. He parked in front of the house and turned off the lights. "Don't want to wake your grandmother."

"Don't worry. Her room is in the back."

She turned toward him. "Thank you for dinner. I had a wonderful time."

"Me too."

He leaned toward her. "I know I crossed over the line a bit tonight."

She interrupted him. "Please don't apologize. It was just as much my fault as yours."

"I wasn't going to apologize for what almost happened between us. I'm not sorry for kissing you the way I did either. I was about to tell you I'd like to see you again and suggest we relax the rules, enjoy each other's company and see where things go."

Beth smiled. "I'm not sorry either. It was foolish of me to set boundaries. I was just afraid."

"Afraid of me?"

"Yes."

"Why?"

She looked away from him. "Because I'm attracted to you."

"And now?"

She turned and faced him again. "I'm terrified."

Ted raised her hand to his lips and kissed her fingertips. "We'll take things slow. I promise I won't pressure you."

"Thank you."

"So, we're good?"

"Very good," she whispered, as he closed the gap between them.

He pushed her hair back and nipped at her ear. She felt that flutter in her stomach, just before their lips touched. Her heart beat a little faster. She'd been deprived of such feelings for way too long. Not wanting it to end, she savored every second of his kisses and clung to him in the darkness. For the moment, Beth forgot about being confused or afraid and thought only of Ted.

When he pulled away, she was disappointed. "Is something wrong?"

He chuckled. "It's after midnight, Cinderella. Come on, I'll walk you to your door."

"I guess I'd better let the charming prince go home before his Mercedes turns into a pumpkin."

He held the copy of his play, while Beth dug for her keys. She unlocked the door and took back the manuscript. He gave her one last, long, lingering kiss. "Think about what I said."

"I will. Good night, Ted."

"Good night. I'll call you," he said, before she went inside.

Beth switched off the porch light, removed her shoes and tip-toed upstairs to her bedroom. She dropped her purse and heels next to the chair and Ted's play on her desk. *I'll read it tomorrow with my coffee out by the bay.*

Still feeling the sensation of Ted's lips on hers, she went into the bathroom to brush her teeth and remove her makeup. Seeing the smudged lipstick, Beth was glad Ann wasn't still up when she came in. *I would have had a hard time explaining that one.*

After changing into her pajamas, she plugged her phone into the charger on the nightstand and crawled into bed. Just as she reached up to snap off the lamp, her phone buzzed. *Who would text me at this hour? I hope nothing is wrong with one of the kids.* Grabbing the phone, Beth smiled when she saw who the message was from.

Pleasant dreams, Cinderella.

She laughed and texted him back.

Good night my charming prince.

Beth put the phone back on the charger and turned off the light. She fluffed her pillow and pulled the sheet over herself. As she drifted off to sleep, thoughts of the handsome playwright filled her head. *When he kissed me out by the bay, he seemed reserved. Almost cautious. Tonight, his kisses were intense. Maybe brandy made him more daring. No, that wasn't it. Ted Lamont's a man who knows what he wants and goes after it. No wonder the man can write such a good love scene.*

* * *

Ted

It was a little after midnight when Ted got back from driving Beth home. Too keyed up to sleep, he got a bottle of water from the fridge, turned on the TV and stretched his long legs out on the couch. He kept seeing images of Beth in that sexy black dress. *She looked fantastic. I wonder if she's asleep yet.* He sent her a text and smiled at her response.

When feelings of guilt hit him, his smile quickly vanished. He looked at the picture of her he had taken on the bench out at the bay. *What will she think when she finds out the woman her ex-husband had an affair with eight years ago was my ex-wife and that I figured it out and didn't say anything? She might even think I knew from the beginning and was trying to even the score? As far as I'm concerned, it's all in the past and should be left there. She might feel differently. Telling her could jeopardize our relationship. If I don't tell her and she somehow finds out, she'll never trust me.*

It's almost one o'clock. I need to think about how I'm going to handle this. But right now, I have to get some sleep. He got off the couch, put the empty bottle in the recycle bin and headed upstairs. "Alexa, turn off the light."

Chapter 13

Beth

It was almost eight o'clock when Beth walked into the kitchen on Saturday morning. Ann was buttering a muffin. "Late night?" asked Ann.

"Later than I'm used to. I didn't get to bed until after midnight."

Ann looked up. "Then I assume you had a good time."

Beth smiled. "Wonderful."

"Coffee will be ready in a minute. Have a muffin with me."

Beth was eager to get started on Ted's play, but she didn't want to hurt Ann's feelings. "Okay, but only for a few minutes. I want to go out by the bay. I have some reading to do."

"And some thinking, I imagine."

She took a homemade corn muffin out of the basket. "You know me too well."

"What is that you have there?"

"It's the play Ted gave Will for the theater. I told him I'd read it."

Ann got them both a cup of coffee. "That was nice of you."

"It's a Christmas play. He's waiting for the Board's approval."

"I'm sure they will jump at the chance to do a Ted Lamont play."

Beth added milk to her cup. "He wants me to audition for the lead."

"Oh?"

"I haven't made any promises."

"But you are at least considering it, aren't you?"

She sighed. "I don't know what to do. It's been years since I've been on a stage. Ted and Will both want me to audition. In fact, I'm meeting Will for lunch today. I'm sure he'll bring it up."

The older woman looked straight at her. "And what do you want?"

Beth couldn't lie to Ann. "I want to do it. Annie, it's the play I saw on Broadway that time I went to New York with my girlfriends. It's a great part and I know all the songs."

"So, what's holding you back?"

"I'm afraid I'm not good enough and that it will put Ted in a tough position if he has to give the part to someone else."

Ann put her hand on Beth's. "Ted Lamont is a professional. The man knows what he's doing. He wouldn't have suggested it if he didn't think you could do it."

"I told him I'd think about it."

"I'll fill your thermal mug so you can get out there and read."

"Thanks, Annie."

Beth got up, put her dishes in the sink, picked up Ted's manuscript and headed for the bay.

The sun was shining, but the morning air was still cool. Beth zipped her jacket and opened the manuscript to the title page. MISTLETOE MADNESS by Ted Lamont. *I'll never forget how excited I felt when the curtain went up or the thunderous sound of applause at the end. That night made me realize how much I loved the theater and wonder if I would ever perform on stage again.*

She took a sip of coffee and began reading ACT I. Beth smiled as she remembered the story of Lorna Hollingsworth and Jack Slater. *I can't believe I'm holding a Ted Lamont play in my hands and thinking about auditioning for the part of Lorna.*

Beth read most of the first act, stopping every so often to read the lines out loud. In ACT II, she skipped ahead to the part where Jack kissed Lorna under the mistletoe. It was a romantic scene with a hot kiss. She imagined Ted writing it and thought about the way he kissed her last night. *I wonder how much of his real kisses he puts into his writing, or is it the other way around?*

When she finished looking over the script, Beth unzipped her jacket, sat back in the bench and stared out at the ocean. She thought about Ted and wondered if he called Diana. *Not that it's any of my business, but I'm curious about why she was so upset with him. I still think it was over more than an unreturned phone call. He thinks she wants something from him. What if she wants him back? How can I compete with a beautiful Hollywood actress?*

Beth looked down at the pages in her lap. *Can I do this? Am I good enough to play Lorna? Ted seems to think so.* She remembered what he said to her. "If you could play Sandy, you can do Lorna."

But can I? Sandy was a long time ago. Carl always said it was a good thing I got married because I never would have made a living as an actress.

Thinking about her ex made Beth angry. *Maybe not, but I could have made one as an interior decorator and he made sure that didn't happen either.*

She picked up the manuscript and held it against her chest. *Ted's right. I can't let Carl take this away from me. I owe it to myself to at least try.*

Chapter 14

Ted

Ted cursed out loud as he maneuvered his way through the Saturday afternoon traffic in Boston. "Damn! Why'd I let her talk me into meeting for lunch?"

He thought about his on again, off again romance with actress Diana Lange. *Not that it was much of a romance. It was always on when she needed me for something and off when she found greener pastures. We dated almost five years and broke up at least four times.*

Ted remembered the first time he saw her eight years ago. It was the day she auditioned for the part of Ava in his new play, *It's Never Enough.* At thirty-one, the voluptuous redhead was no longer a box-office draw. Diana had decided to give up her waning movie career and return to the theater. *The director didn't think she was right for the part. I disagreed. I should have stayed out of it. Little did I know how well the title fit her. Nothing was ever enough for that woman. What does she want from me now?*

When Ted entered the bar at the Four Seasons Hotel, Diana was waiting for him. She waved in his direction. "Over here, Teddy."

As if I could miss that mass of coppery curls. May as well get this over with. He walked over to where she was seated.

"Hello, Diana."

She flashed him a smile he was only too familiar with. "Thank you for coming, Ted."

He didn't comment.

She put her drink down on the bar. "Don't I even get a hug?"

Her pretty green eyes showed no traces of the venom that was in them last night. He leaned forward and put his arms around her. "Of course."

She hugged him and kissed his cheek. "That wasn't so hard, was it?"

He pulled out the chair and sat next to her. "What's that you're drinking?"

"An Appletini. Would you like a sip?"

What I'd like is a Jack Daniels on the rocks, but I'm driving. "No thanks. That's a little too strong for me."

He signaled the bartender and ordered a glass of white wine."

"Looks like that home-town girlfriend of yours has changed your taste in a lot of things."

He knew she was baiting him. "Diana, you're a beautiful woman until your claws come out. And while we're on the subject, you were totally out of line last night."

She sipped her drink and looked at him again. Her attitude shifted quickly. "I'm sorry. You're right about last night, of course. I was angry that you didn't return my phone call and when I saw you with a date, I guess I got a bit jealous."

"Jealous! We broke up three years ago. And, by the way, don't you have a husband somewhere?"

"That's been over for a while now."

The bartender brought his drink. "Why am I not surprised?"

"Oh, Ted, please let's not argue. Can't we just enjoy our drinks and catch up?"

She's calling me Ted. Oh, she's after something all right. "I'm not here to hash over old times. You said you wanted to talk to me about something. Why don't we get a table, so we can get to it?"

"I thought we could have lunch in my room. That would give us some privacy."

"You got a room?"

"I told you I was staying in Boston."

That kind of privacy I don't need. What the hell is she after? "I'll get us a table."

She lifted her empty glass and signaled the bartender for another. "Charge these to my room."

Ted returned with the hostess. "They have a private table in a quiet corner for us."

"Terrific."

Now who's being sarcastic? He helped her off the chair and picked up his drink. Together they followed the hostess to the table.

Ted ordered another wine with his meal. He had a feeling he was going to need a second drink.

Things remained friendly over the shrimp cocktail. Diana told him she had moved back to New York about six months ago. She asked about his new house and how he liked living in a small town. "It's so not you. Don't you miss Broadway and the theater?"

"No. I love living near the ocean. I get to see my daughter more now."

"What about your writing? Don't you want to write plays anymore?"

He shrugged. "I'm writing for television now. I can do that from anywhere."

"I heard you were doing that."

79

So, she knows what I'm doing now. Mystery solved.

It was perfect timing that the waiter showed up with lunch just then. It gave him a chance to avoid the subject so he could eat. "It looks delicious."

She spread her napkin across her lap. "Yes. I'm hungry."

Diana didn't mention it again while they were eating. Instead, she reminisced about the past. "A lot has happened in the past eight years. You gave me my first big break in the theater. I'll always be grateful for that."

"You're a talented actress. You could be difficult and temperamental, but you were never late for rehearsals and you always knew your lines. You deserved it."

"I remember a certain director who didn't agree with you when I auditioned."

Ted smiled. "He wanted a blonde for the lead. I wanted the redhead who was sitting in the front row."

"You sure did."

They both laughed. He had forgotten the sensuous laugh Diana had when she was being genuine. *But is she being genuine now, or is she acting?*

Ted was enjoying the lunch in spite of himself. So much so, that he allowed himself to get distracted. For a few minutes, he forgot she was after something.

"How long are you in town for?"

"It depends."

Oh, oh. Here it comes. If it depends on me, she'll be on the next flight back to wherever she came from because whatever it is, I'm not interested. "Are you going to tell me, or do I have to guess?"

"What do you mean?"

"Just what is it you want, Diana?"

80

She put her fork down and looked straight at him. Her green eyes softened. "I want a part in one of your TV movies."

So that's it. I should have figured that out. "Diana, you've never worked in television. It's different than the theater or the movies."

"How is it different? Acting is acting. A movie is a movie. You said yourself I'm a talented actress."

"I don't have that kind of power in the media."

"You're Ted Lamont. You write the movies. You have power."

"I'm sorry, Diana. I can't help you this time."

She motioned to the server for another drink. "You mean you won't help me."

"No. I really can't. I only write the movies."

"You could introduce me to the right people. You could have a party and invite some of the producers."

Ted didn't like where this was going. He didn't want to get involved with Diana on any level. *All this being grateful for the big break I gave her was just her way of playing me.*

"I'm sorry."

"You're just trying to get even with me for the way I acted in front of your girlfriend last night.

People were beginning to look at them. "Please lower your voice. It has nothing to do with that."

She pleaded with him. "Ted, I need to work."

"What about that producer ex-husband of yours? He must know people. Get him to help you. Go back to the theater."

She took a long swallow of her drink. "So, after all we've meant to each other, you won't help me?"

"I'm not working on anything that has a part suitable for you right now."

"You mean I'm too old."

He rubbed his forehead. "No. That's not what I meant at all."

She leaned forward. "Being in one of your TV movies would give my career just what it needs right now. Please say you'll help me. I'll do anything you want."

He was getting a headache. "I'll ask around."

She smiled and reached across the table for his hand. "Oh Ted. Thank you."

"I'm not making any promises, but I'll ask a couple of people and let them know you are interested in getting into TV movies."

She squeezed his hand. "Thank you, Ted. That's all I ask."

Tears filled her eyes. Whether they were real tears or not, he hadn't a clue. *All she asks.*

He finished his wine and reached for the check. She stopped him. "Lunch is on me. I invited you, remember?"

He stood up. "Thank you. I really have to leave now."

She got up, wrapped her arms around his neck and kissed him. "Are you sure you wouldn't like to come up to my room?"

He reached up, circled his fingers around her wrists and pulled her arms away. "I'll be in touch."

Chapter 15

Ted

It was after three when Ted got home from Boston. His lunch with Diana turned into an exhausting ordeal that left him with a colossal headache. *I should have known what she wanted. Why did I let myself get sucked into her drama? I'll make a few calls, as promised, and then be done with her.*

He needed to catch up on some work, but a nap seemed like a better idea. He downed two Tylenol, sprawled out on the couch and pulled out his phone. There were two messages. One was from Will Donaldson. The other one was Beth. He listened to hers first.

"Hi Ted. It's Beth. I'm sure you've heard from Will by now. Call me when you can."

I wonder if she's decided to audition.

Next, he listened to Will's message.

"Hey, Ted. Will Donaldson. Good news. The Board is thrilled at having a Ted Lamont play and love that it's a Christmas theme. Call me when you get a chance. We can talk about getting the word out and auditions and set design. Had lunch with Beth. She's going to help with set designs and whatever else we need her for."

"We need her for the leading role," he said out loud.

Unable to reach Will, Ted left him a voicemail and called Beth.

"Ted, hi! Have you spoken to Will yet?"

"No. We've been playing phone tag. But he left me a message that the Board approved the play."

"I didn't doubt for a minute they would. Why wouldn't they jump at the chance? And having you around to help is a big bonus."

Ted rubbed the middle of his forehead. "Sweetheart, can we talk a little later?"

"I'm sorry. You probably have work to do."

"I do, but I wanted to return your call."

"Ted, is something wrong? You sound a little strange."

"To be honest, I have a headache and I need to lie down for a while."

"Oh, I'm sorry. We can talk tomorrow."

He didn't want her to hang up yet. "Wait. Are you free tonight? I could pick you up around seven and we could go to the Black Rock for burgers and celebrate."

"Are you sure you're up to it?"

"I'll be fine once the Tylenol kicks in, and I take a nap. I'd really like to see you."

"All right, then. I'd love to."

"Beth…Will said you agreed to help with set designs. Have you made any other decisions?"

She hesitated. "Why don't we talk about that tonight? See you at seven."

He shut off his phone, put his head on the pillow and closed his eyes. *I can't tell Beth what I know about Carl and Cynthia tonight. I have a feeling she decided to audition and wants to tell me in person. I don't want to ruin that for her. I'll figure out a way to tell her later. Right now, I have to get rid of this headache.*

Two hours later, Ted woke up feeling much better. He turned his phone back on and checked his messages. *Great. Now Diana has my cell number. I should have called her on the house phone this morning. I wasn't thinking.*

Thank you for meeting with me today. Hope to hear from you soon.

He sent back a quick reply and left it at that.

Thanks for lunch. I'll be in touch.

He made a quick call to Will Donaldson. They made arrangements to meet at the theater early next week to talk about the auditions. "I'm seeing Beth later. Maybe we have our leading lady."

* * *

Beth

When Beth got off the phone, she couldn't shake the feeling that whatever was bothering Ted was more than a headache. *He didn't mention where he'd been all afternoon. Maybe he was with Diana. I didn't dare ask if he called her back. It's really none of my business.*

She sat at her desk and looked down at the copy of *Mistletoe Madness. He didn't seem all that thrilled about Will's news either. What did I expect? The man is used to Broadway. But he did ask if I've made any decisions. I think he'll be happy when I tell him I'm going to audition for the part of Lorna. Will was certainly excited.*

Beth thought about her lunch with Will Donaldson. She enjoyed reminiscing with him about when they were young.

"I always loved it when you spent time with your grandparents in the summer. Annie would send you out with some of her pink lemonade. I'd drink it real slow, so you'd stay and talk to me."

Beth adored the tall, muscular boy with sandy blonde hair, blue eyes and an incredible tan. He was much more interesting than boys her own age. "And my grandmother would stand in the doorway and tell me to come in and let you get your work done. She thought you had a crush on me and that you were too old."

Will's expression changed. He looked straight at her. "Josephine was right. I was crazy about you. But you were fifteen and I was eighteen. She was right about that too. I **was** too old for you...then. But I thought it was because she didn't want you to date the boy who mowed her lawn."

"Oh, no. That wasn't it at all. She thought of me as still a child and you as a man with a bit of a wild streak."

Will laughed. "I could have gone to jail just for what I was thinking back then. By the time you were old enough for me to date legally, I was away at college. When I came home, you were in college."

"Then you got engaged."

"And by the time I was divorced, you were married to Carl. Our timing never seemed to be right, did it?"

Beth smiled. "No, it wasn't."

Will reached across the table and touched her hand. "I'm sorry your marriage ended, Beth. But it's great to have you back in Tucker's Landing."

"Thank you, Will. And please promise me you won't tell Ted that I'm going to try out for the part. I want to tell him myself."

Will pulled his hand away. "There's that rotten timing again."

Chapter 16

Ted

Beth looked the picture of summer in an ice blue tank top and long, white gauze skirt. Ted couldn't resist giving her a quick kiss on the cheek. "You look beautiful. That color looks great on you."

She was all smiles. "Thank you."

He caught the light scent of her perfume, as he helped slip the matching lace shawl over her shoulders. "Our reservation is for 7:30."

Eager to hear Beth's decision, he led her to his car. When he got in, Ted turned toward her before starting the engine. "I'm sorry if I sounded impatient on the phone this afternoon. My head was throbbing."

"No need to apologize. I'm glad you're feeling better."

He was thankful she didn't ask what gave him the headache or where he'd been all afternoon. *I wouldn't want to lie about it, but no need to bring Diana up and chance ruining our evening.* "The nap helped."

Ted wondered why Beth hadn't mention her lunch with Will or anything about the play on the way to the Black Rock. *Probably waiting till we get to the restaurant.*

They were seated right away at a corner booth with good sightlines of the ocean. He slid in beside her "I requested a booth, so we'd have more privacy."

"This is nice. Such a gorgeous view."

"Yes. It's relaxing."

Once they settled in, Ted opened the wine list. "Champagne tonight?" he asked.

She looked back at him. "I'd rather have white wine, if you don't mind."

He put the list back on the table. "Of course."

Maybe she doesn't think champagne goes with cheeseburgers. When the server came, he ordered two glasses of Pinot Grigio.

"I know I said burgers, but you can order anything you want."

He was glad to see her smiling again. "Oh, I'm okay with that. I had a big lunch."

"And how was your lunch with Will?"

"It was fun. We reminisced about the past and got caught up on what's new in Tucker's Landing."

He drummed his fingers on the table. "That's right. You two go back a long way."

"Yes. I remember when he mowed lawns and did landscaping to earn money for college. He ended up with his own landscaping business. His sons pretty much run it now. That's how he has time to manage the little theater."

"From what I've seen, he does a great job of it. He was happy the Board agreed with him on the play."

"Yes. He's very excited about it."

She must be afraid to tell me her decision. "I'm sorry, Beth. I shouldn't have assumed we were celebrating. I take it you've decided not to audition."

Her eyes brightened. "No. I mean, yes! I've decided to go for it."

Ted shook his head. "You mean you **are** going to audition?"

"Yes. You were right. I can't let Carl take this away from me."

He moved closer and gave her a big hug. "Why didn't you tell me sooner?"

"I wanted to tell you the minute we got in your car, but you didn't seem too excited on the phone about the play being approved, so I was a little nervous about it."

"Believe me Beth, that had nothing to do with the play. I'm thrilled that you want to audition for the leading role. But why not the champagne?"

"For one thing, I haven't got the part yet. I don't feel right celebrating."

Ted knew there was more. He had an idea of where this was going. "I'm okay with that. Is something else bothering you?"

Beth hesitated. "I don't want this to get in the way of our friendship."

"It won't."

She continued. "I don't want any special consideration. You have to promise to tell me if I'm not good enough."

"I wish you'd stop doubting yourself."

She lowered her eyes. "I wouldn't want people to think I got the part because…"

He stopped her. "You're afraid they might think you got it because we're more than friends?"

"Well…yes."

"I don't care what other people think. Not about me anyway. But I do have respect for your feelings. Beth, there's something you need to understand."

She looked back at him. "What's that?"

He took her hands in his. "I'm a professional. Contrary to what you might have read in the tabloids, no actress has ever landed a part in one of my plays who hasn't deserved it on her own merit."

"Oh, Ted, I don't doubt your professionalism."

"Then what makes you think I'd start with you? Do you honestly believe I'd set you up to fail? That I'd put you on stage if I thought you didn't have the talent to be there? Do you think I'd risk hurting the play and my reputation?"

Beth smiled and leaned closer to him. "I know you wouldn't do that. But you don't know if I have any talent yet."

Ted laughed. "It wasn't hard to find the reviews from that South Shore performance of yours. And I don't care what Carl told you, no critic writes a review to be nice. Besides, both Will and your grandmother say you have a beautiful voice."

"Don't you think they might be just a little biased?"

"Maybe Will, but I wouldn't dare doubt Josephine's opinion."

Ted held up his glass. "Is it okay to make a toast to your decision?"

Beth reached for her drink and smiled. "I'd say that alone is worthy of a toast."

Chapter 17

Ted

On the way home from the Black Rock, Ted mulled over his thoughts about Beth's decision. *I hope I was right to encourage her on this. What if I'm wrong. How could I tell her she's not right for the part? She could end up hating me. I'd hate myself.*

"Why so quiet?" asked Beth.

Her question surprised him. "Just thinking how happy I am about your decision."

"I was afraid you were having second thoughts."

Ted pulled into his driveway, shut the engine off and turned to face her. "No second thoughts. No doubts. And you shouldn't be having any either."

"Thank you for helping me get my confidence back."

"It's always been there, Beth. You just needed to be reminded of it."

In the darkness, he saw her inviting lips curve into a smile. When he leaned forward and kissed her, Ted knew he had nothing to worry about. *I've always trusted my instincts. My gut tells me she's good...at a lot of things.*

Ted was eager to talk more about the play with Beth, but mostly he just wanted to be with her. As much as he liked kissing her, doing it in a parked car in his driveway wasn't his style. "It's getting hot in the car. Why don't we go in?"

"Yeah. No need to give the neighbors something to talk about."

"We can have a drink and look over the script. You can tell me which scenes are your favorites."

Once they were inside, he led her to the living room. She dropped her copy of the manuscript on the coffee table and giggled when a lamp came on with Ted's command.

"She's so obedient."

He walked toward her, smiling. "That's the way I like my women."

"Sorry. I'm not about to make that mistake again."

Ted put both arms around her. "You know I'm kidding, right? I like you just the way you are."

He was about to take up where he left off in the car, when the house phone rang.

"Do you want to answer that?" Beth asked.

"Let it go to the machine. I'm busy."

His lips covered hers, as he pulled her close to him. His greeting played in the background.

"You've reached the home of Ted Lamont. Sorry I'm unable to take your call right now. Please leave your name and number after the beep and I'll get back to you as soon as possible."

He heard the long beep and felt Beth stiffen at the sound of the voice.

"You don't seem to be answering your phones, Teddy dear. I just want to tell you I enjoyed lunch today. Maybe next time you can stay longer. Don't forget your promise. Call me."

Beth pulled away from him. "I guess that explains the headache."

Damn you, Diana! "Beth, I can explain."

"Don't be silly. You don't owe me any explanations. It's not my business where you go or who you go there with."

"I was going to tell you. Really. I didn't want to bring it up at dinner and ruin the evening."

The smile she gave him could have frozen water. "That was sweet of you, Ted."

Why did I let the machine take that call? Oh yeah. I was preoccupied. "Why don't you make yourself comfortable on the sofa and I'll get us some brandy?"

She moved toward the sofa. "Good idea. I could use a drink."

When he came back, Ted handed her a glass and sat down next to her. "I'm sorry about that, Beth."

She took the brandy snifter from him. "It's okay. I over-reacted. I guess I was a bit surprised that's all."

Ted took a drink before he told her his reason for having lunch with Diana. "I had no idea she was staying at the Four Seasons when I agreed to meet her for lunch."

"So, she invited you to her hotel."

"It was not what you're thinking. I swear. We ate in the restaurant. I only went so I could find out what she wants from me."

"And did you?"

"Oh yes."

Beth ran her finger over the rim of her glass. "So, you were right?"

"She wants me to get her a part in one of my TV movies."

"And you promised her you would."

"No. I tried to tell her I don't have that kind of power. I only write the stories."

She tilted her head. "But she said you made her a promise."

"No. I told her I couldn't make any promises. All I said was I would make a couple of phone calls and I'd be in touch."

"That's all?"

"I didn't go up to her room, if that's what you're wondering. Arguing with her gave me a massive headache. I couldn't get out of there fast enough."

"I'm sorry, Ted. I have no right."

"Beth...we've already established that we can't keep things between us at a friendship level. You have every right to know if I'm involved with anyone else."

"I guess I should have just come out and asked you."

"It's my fault. I should have told you about lunch. Beth, I hope you believe me when I tell you I'm not involved with anyone and I'm not seeing anyone else. And that includes Diana Lange."

"I believe you."

"Good."

He smiled and made an obvious attempt to change the subject. "Tell me more about your new job with Valerie. In the restaurant you mentioned starting Monday."

Beth sat back against the soft pillows. "Yes. We're going to go over the details of an open house she'd like me to stage. She'll show me some pictures and I'll tell her my ideas."

"You sound excited about it."

"I am. I'm happy to have a job that involves decorating. Plus, I'm looking forward to working with Val."

"I can tell you first-hand, the woman knocks herself out for her clients."

"That she does."

Ted rested one arm on the back of the sofa. "I'm glad I bought this house...for a lot of reasons."

Beth smiled. "It's a great location. Val says you have a gorgeous view from your deck."

"Yes. I can see the ocean. Nice view of your brother's house too, by the way."

She laughed. "Val told me that too."

"I'm pretty much settled in now. What about you? Are you feeling more at home?"

"Yes. I love being with my grandmother and Annie and it's good to be able to see Dylan and my nephew again. Keith is a wonderful young man."

"Dylan's son, right? I've met him and his girlfriend, Jessie."

"They're a cute couple. Jessie's mom works for Val."

"No wonder you feel at home. You already know everyone in town."

"Being around family has helped a lot."

He nodded. "I know what you mean. I like living close to my daughter. Can I freshen your drink or get you something else? Coffee maybe?"

"No, thanks. I'll nurse this one."

Ted put his glass on the coffee table. "Me too. I have to drive you home later."

He reached over, picked up the script and started thumbing through it. "Let's talk about the play. Would you like to go over some lines together?"

Beth took a small sip of her drink before she answered. "All right."

He handed it to Beth and stood up. "I'll go get another copy. Be right back."

When he returned, Ted sat down next to Beth. "I'll read Jack's lines. Why don't we start with Lorna telling Jack she's accepted another position?"

Beth put her drink down and sat at the edge of the sofa facing Ted. "Okay."

He opened the script to one of several pages with blue sticky notes. "ACT I, Scene III. Jack has just come back from a meeting. Lorna tells him she needs to speak to him and follows him into his office. He sits behind his desk. She sits facing him. You start."

* * *

Beth

Beth looked down at the page. She took a deep breath and let it out. *Focus on the lines, not on who I'm reading with. This isn't the audition. We're just reading lines.*

Once the words started coming out, she became more relaxed. When they finished reading the scene, Ted was smiling. *Well, that's a good sign.* "How'd I do?"

"You did great."

"Is that your professional opinion, or your biased one?"

He laughed. "A little of both. Professionally, I could sense your nervousness on the first few lines. However, once you got into it, you did great. You didn't mess up one line. I could feel Lorna's mixed emotions about telling Jack she was leaving."

"Thank you. You're right. I suddenly realized I was reading a scene from a Ted Lamont play **with** Ted Lamont."

His smile faded. His expression turned serious. "That's understandable. But I don't want you to feel uncomfortable or nervous. This isn't an audition. It's just you and me reading a few lines in the privacy of my living room. You're not on stage and you don't need to impress Ted Lamont."

He smiled again. "Trust me. He's already quite taken with you."

Beth felt the redness on her cheeks. "It's very sweet of you to do this with me."

96

"I'm enjoying it. Let's try one or two more and end with the kiss under the mistletoe in the second act."

She started flipping pages in the script. *I hope I can remember it's Jack Slater I'm kissing.*

* * *

Ted

They read two more scenes. She read every line perfectly and didn't seem nervous at all. *Yup. My instincts were right again. I think we have our Lorna.*

"What do you say? Want to tackle the mistletoe scene and stop at that for tonight?"

"All right."

Ted stood up. "Let's go under a doorway to give us the setting."

"Imagine mistletoe hanging over us." They stood under the archway to the living room and read the lines leading up to the kiss.

"Okay. Now, Jack puts his arms around Lorna. She tries to push him away."

LORNA: "Jack! What are you doing?"

JACK: "It's okay. We're under the mistletoe."

LORNA: "What?"

(Lorna looks up and sees the mistletoe.)

JACK: "Merry Christmas, Lorna."

(Jack takes her in his arms and starts to kiss her.)

Beth dropped the script. It hit the floor with a loud thud. "I'm sorry. Holding the manuscript was awkward. It threw me off."

Ted picked it up and put it aside. "My fault. I should have thought of that. The way Lorna reacts to Jack's kiss can make or break this scene. You couldn't put your arms around me with a book in your hands. Let's try it again. Without the distraction."

Beth looked up. This time, when Ted's lips touched hers, she leaned into him and reacted by giving him a long, smoldering kiss. Her lips were soft and tasted of brandy. He pulled her closer and began kissing her neck.

"Ted. This isn't in the script."

His voice was muffled. "I forgot my lines. I'm ad-libbing."

"Maybe I need to concentrate more on who I'm supposed to be kissing."

He continued to gently kiss her neck. "I'd rather you didn't think about Jack Slater when you're kissing me."

"Trust me. I wasn't thinking about Jack when I kissed you."

He whispered in her ear. "Would you like to see the view from my deck?"

"In the dark?"

He gave her another long kiss. "If you spend the night, I could show you the view in the morning."

She smiled. "Imagine Dylan looking up and seeing me here first thing in the morning."

"I'm not worried about your brother."

"What about my grandmother. You want to explain to her why I didn't come home all night?"

Ted sighed. "I forgot about Josephine. I guess you'll have to come for lunch some afternoon to see it."

She looked up at him. "You know…it's a clear night. I'll bet the view of the stars over the ocean is lovely."

He kissed her forehead, turned and led her upstairs to his bedroom and out onto the deck. It was a beautiful starlit summer night. A gentle breeze rustled through the trees. The moon, not quite full, hung over the ocean.

Beth stood close to the railing. "Val was right. It's very pretty up here."

He wrapped his arms around her waist and stood behind her. "We should be able to find the Big Dipper easy tonight."

"Dylan has a telescope. Val said he showed her the stars the first time she went to his house."

"And you were worried about what your brother would think?"

She laughed and turned to face him. He was staring at her.

"What are you thinking right now?" she asked.

He answered without hesitating. "That I want to make love to you."

When she didn't answer, Ted thought he'd gone too far. "Does that make you uncomfortable?"

Her eyes danced in the moonlight. "If it did, we'd still be in your living room."

Keeping one arm around Beth's waist, Ted turned toward the sliders. "Let's go in."

He shut the door and closed the blinds.

He walked her over to the bed and switched off the lamp.

"No Alexa in here?" she teased.

Ted turned to face her. He pulled her against him. "There's no one in here except you and me. Some things I like to do for myself."

She undid the top two buttons on his shirt. "Are you sure I can't help just a little?"

"You're driving me crazy."

"Want me to stop?"

"Hell, no."

Ted watched her slowly unfasten the rest of the buttons. He felt her lips brushing across his bare chest. Gently, he raised the silky tank top over her head. She slid her arms around his waist and leaned into him. Her skin was soft and warm.

He took off his shirt, turned down the covers and took her in his arms again. "Let's work on that kiss now."

Chapter 18

Beth

Beth sat at the kitchen table with both hands wrapped around her favorite coffee mug. Images of Ted and last night floated through her head like sequences of a dream as she watched the steam swirl from the hot liquid.

It couldn't have been a dream, she thought. *I can still feel the heat from his body and hear his voice cutting through the darkness.*

"It's getting late, Cinderella. I better get you home."

"Just a few more minutes," she whispered.

"Whatever you want, Princess." He rolled toward her and gave her a long, lingering kiss.

Beth took a sip of coffee and put her cup back down. She closed her eyes. *If it was a dream, I don't want to wake up.*

Beth's thoughts were suddenly interrupted. "No coffee out by the bay this morning?"

Startled by Ann's voice, she looked up. "What? Oh, no. I got home late."

Ann made herself a cup of tea. "I know."

So much for sneaking into the house at almost two in the morning. "I'm sorry. Did I wake you?"

The older woman smiled. "No. I was watching an old movie that ended at one and you weren't home yet. Those must have been some burgers."

"What do you mean?"

Ann brought her tea over to the table and sat down. "You said Ted was taking you to the Black Rock for burgers."

101

Beth got defensive. "He did."

"I was teasing, not judging. I was young once too, you know."

She hadn't meant it to come out that way. "I'm sorry. He invited me back to his place to talk about the script."

"So, you told him you've decided to audition."

"Yes."

"I'll bet he was happy about it."

Beth's eyes opened all the way for the first time that morning. "He was thrilled. We read some scenes together."

"If one of them was that scene under the mistletoe, you must have it perfect by now."

Her mouth flew open. "Annie!"

Ann took a sip of her tea. "Don't look so shocked. You think I never tip-toed up those stairs in the wee hours of the morning?"

They quickly changed the subject when they heard the tapping of Josephine's cane just near the kitchen.

Ann got up to make her a cup of tea. "Good morning, Josephine. You're just in time to have muffins with us."

"Good morning, Gram. Did you sleep well?"

The old woman sat next to Beth and looked from one to the other. "Better than either of you, I'm sure."

Beth gave Ann a quick sideways glance. "Have a muffin, Gram. They're delicious."

"No need to change the subject on my account. I take it you ladies were discussing my granddaughter's late-night activities."

"Why do you say that Josephine?"

"Because my dear, you watch movies until all hours. I doubt you would have stopped when you heard me coming if you were talking about a movie."

She turned toward Beth. "You, on the other hand, had a date, which I'm sure was more interesting."

"I'm sorry if I woke you when I came in."

"Don't be silly. I can't hear anything from my room and without my hearing aids."

Beth looked confused. "Then why do you think I came home late?"

"How many times do I have to tell you, I'm old but not feeble minded. I have a very good memory. You're not the only one who has ever tried to sneak in this house in the middle of the night and not wake me."

Ann choked on her tea.

Josephine turned toward her. "I was referring to my daughter."

Beth couldn't imagine her mother ever doing such things. "My mother? Mom did that?"

"The only difference is, I could hear her. With you, the smile on your face is a dead giveaway. Not to mention, you look like hell. Butter me one of those muffins, please and then I want to hear about your date with the charming playwright."

Beth stifled a laugh and looked at Ann. They both shrugged their shoulders. She buttered a blueberry muffin for Josephine and told her about their meal at the Black Rock and about her evening with Ted, leaving out the best part.

Josephine smiled with delight. "I can't wait to see you on the stage."

"I don't have the part yet, Gram."

"Ted Lamont knows talent when he sees it."

"He hasn't seen me act."

"Didn't you say you went over lines together last night?"

"Yes, but that was just reading lines."

"Sounds to me like the man wants you for his leading lady."

"Ted's only helping with the play. His input will carry a lot of weight, but Will Donaldson has the final say."

"Will would put you in the play in a minute."

"Thanks for the vote of confidence, but I still have to audition like everyone else."

Josephine reached out and touched her hand. "You'll do fine, I'm sure."

Beth got up and gave her grandmother a hug. "I'll be in my room. I have some things to catch up on and I need to go through my closet. I'm working with Val tomorrow and I have no idea what to wear."

"Oh, I almost forgot. You're starting your new job tomorrow. Nice to see you doing some decorating again."

"Yes. It will be fun for you," said Ann. "Do you think you might get back into it at some point?"

"Oh, I don't know, Annie. I've toyed with the idea of having my own business and taking on one client at a time maybe."

Josephine perked up. "When you're ready, I have a customer for you."

"Really? Who?"

"Ann's rooms could use a coat of paint. She's been wanting to replace the curtains and linens and do something about the chair. I'm sure you could come up with some good ideas. I'd be happy to pay for it."

Ann looked at Josephine. "That's very generous of you."

"You've got a birthday coming up. Consider it my gift to you."

Ann looked at Beth. "If you're too busy it can wait until you have the time."

"The timing is perfect. It'll be at least a month before auditions start and my job with Val is only part-time."

"So long as you're sure you have the time."

"I'm sure. You make a list of what you want to do and the colors you like, and we'll go from there."

"Okay."

Beth hugged her grandmother before heading upstairs. "I thought I'd invite Jamie over for dinner some night next week, if it's okay with you."

Josephine's face lit up. "By all means. I haven't seen that great granddaughter of mine in a while. Her brother stops by often to check on us, but we haven't seen Jamie lately."

"I know. She's been busy with her new job, but she wants to come for a visit."

Ann chimed in. "I'll make a special dinner. Maybe Tom can come too."

"Thanks Annie. I'll ask him. Right now, I have to make a few calls and I need to figure out what to wear tomorrow."

* * *

Alone in her room, Beth sat in her comfortable chair with Ted's manuscript in her lap. Flashbacks of last night took over her thoughts again as she slowly turned the pages. *I still can't believe I was reading lines with Ted Lamont. It was sweet of him to do that with me. He's a kind and considerate man. I'm sure he'll do whatever's best for the play. Working with Ted and being around the theater will be fun and exciting, even if I don't get the part. And if I don't, well at least I tried. I'll be disappointed, but I'll get over it.*

Beth thumbed through the pages and paused when she got to the mistletoe scene. She closed the manuscript and leaned her head back in the chair. *Who am I kidding? I want that part.*

Chapter 19

Ted

Ted walked close to the water along White Stone Beach, mindful of the waves that were rolling toward him. He watched the tiny ripples unfold, spreading white foam across the top of each wave. *It's like fingers floating over a keyboard tapping out a symphony, one note at a time,* he thought, as he breathed in the salt air.

Whenever Ted needed a break from work, he headed for the beautiful stretch of beach that could be seen from his second-floor deck. *Taking a walk in the middle of a workday is one of my favorite perks about living here. A short walk usually clears my mind and rejuvenates me. It doesn't seem to be working today.*

He stopped, bent down and picked up an unusual looking piece of sea glass. *This looks like the stuff Beth collects.* He brushed the sand off and held it in his hand so he could get a better look. Ted eyed it carefully. *Odd shape. Smooth edges. No bigger than a quarter. I don't know what she does with any of it. I think she'd like the deep, sea green color.* He slipped it in his pocket. *And there it is. The reason I can't concentrate on work. Why I couldn't sleep last night. Why I'm stuffing broken glass in my pocket. And why a walk isn't much help. I can't get the woman out of my head.*

He took a deep breath and stared out at the incoming tide. *Why wouldn't I want to think about how good it felt to hold her in my arms and feel her soft skin against mine? The way her eyes closed just before I kissed her. The taste of her lips or the sweet scent of her perfume. I've been dreaming about making love to Beth since the day I kissed her out by the bay. Is it any wonder I can't think of anything else, now that my dreams have become a reality?*

Ted's thoughts were interrupted when a small wave broke over the front of his sneakers. He jumped back quickly, nearly falling over. *I better pay attention before I'm swept out to sea.* He laughed at himself and said out loud. "I can just see the headlines. Lovesick Playwright Drowns While Daydreaming on White Stone Beach."

Moving away from the water, he turned and looked down at his feet. *What in hell am I laughing at? I just ruined a $100 pair of sneakers.* He shoved both hands in his pockets and headed for the path to the sidewalk.

When Ted got home, he went in the back door, took off his sneakers and left them on the mat in the mud room. *Maybe they'll be okay once they dry out.*

He got a bottle of water out of the fridge, went into his office, sat down at the computer and pulled up the script he had been working on earlier. After ten minutes of staring at the screen, he leaned back in the chair and rubbed his eyes. *I'm probably just tired. I had a late night. Didn't get much sleep.*

Ted got up and walked over to the sofa. He put his phone on silent and stretched out on the soft leather with his arms folded over his chest. *Lovesick playwright.* He laughed at himself. *Maybe that's why I can't sleep or concentrate on my work? It's been so long since I've been in love, I might not recognize the symptoms.*

He closed his eyes, but sleep didn't come. Images of Beth reading from a script flashed through his mind. She seemed to be struggling. *She read the lines perfectly with me last night. I hope I didn't talk her into something she's not ready for. No. I'm sure I didn't. I just gave her the encouragement* she needed. *It was a hell of a lot more than that useless excuse of a husband ever did for her. He robbed her of her dreams and destroyed her self-esteem.*

Ted's eyes flew open at the thought of Carl Piedmont. *There it is. That's what's eating at me.* He rolled over onto his side and punched the pillow. *I haven't told Beth that my ex was the woman on Cape Cod who was with her husband eight years ago. And after last night, I don't intend to. It won't do either of us any good. She didn't want to know who the woman was back then. What makes me think she'd want to know now? The past belongs in the past. We've both suffered enough on account of those two. I won't destroy Beth's happiness by dredging up painful memories.*

He gave the pillow another punch, closed his eyes and let his thoughts drift back to last night. *It wouldn't take any effort to fall in love with her. No effort at all.*

October

Chapter 20

Beth

A colorful array of fallen leaves swirled around Beth's ankles as she hurried across the parking lot on the first morning of auditions. The scent of burning firewood, typical of early October, hung in the cool, crisp air. Two big orange pumpkins with theater masks painted on them adorned the wooden steps of the Little Theater. Beth got to the porch and took a deep breath. *Autumn in New England. My favorite time of year.* She opened the door, walked in and spotted Ted. He was standing next to Will with his back to the door. *Oh good. He's talking and doesn't see me. The last thing I need is to be seen with him, or Will for that matter. Although, anyone from around here would think nothing of that. Everyone knows Will.*

After seeing the sign with the big red arrow marked "AUDITIONS – SIGN IN," she headed down the center aisle to the long, wooden table that had been set up near the orchestra section for tryouts. Several people were already seated in the first twelve rows, on the right side, facing the stage, that had been reserved for the performers. Others stood in small groups in the center aisle and in the right outside aisle. The excitement in their voices echoed through the small theater. Beth took her place in line to sign up.

"Hello, Beth," said a woman sitting behind the table. "It's nice to see you. I was thrilled when Will told us you were going to audition for the part of Lorna."

Although there was something familiar about the older woman, Beth had no clue who she was. "I'm sorry but I can't remember your name."

The woman smiled. "It's been a long time since you've seen me. I'm Muriel Donaldson."

"Of course! Mrs. Donaldson. You're Will's Aunt Muriel. I remember. You worked at the library."

"I still do. I'm also on the Board of the theater. I volunteered to help during auditions."

"That's nice of you. Will didn't tell me."

"Probably never thought to mention it. But he mentioned that you were back in Tucker's Landing and that you've also volunteered to help with set designing as well as trying out for the lead in the play."

Beth wondered what else her nephew had mentioned. "That's a man for you."

Mrs. Donaldson handed her a sign-up sheet on a clipboard. "Be sure to fill in which part you are trying out for. Then you may take a seat anywhere in the first twelve rows. Good luck, dear."

"Thank you, Mrs. Donaldson. It was nice to see you."

Beth filled out the form and took an aisle seat in the fifth row. *This theater certainly has changed since Dylan and I came here with Gram when we were kids. The old torn seats have been replaced with comfortable ones with thick cushions. They've done over the dressing rooms and added a small kitchen. Not to mention the new floor on the stage and the new curtain.* She took the script out of her bag, placed it in her lap and sat up straight. *This is good. I have a clear view of the stage and won't have to climb over anyone when it's my turn to go up. It's also far enough away from Ted. Good that he's sitting further back. I'm glad he's here, but it would make me more nervous if he was in the front row.*

Beth tried to rehearse the lines to the second act in her head, but the various conversations going on around her were too distracting. She glanced over in Ted's direction, hoping to get a smile from him that would calm her nerves. He was still talking to Will and had his back to her. *Well, I did tell him not to pay much attention to me during the auditions. He agreed to keep his distance.*

Turning her attention back to the little groups, Beth wondered which actresses were there to audition for the part of Lorna. She tapped her fingers on the script. *Looks like there are more than I expected.*

Two pretty, young women walked up the aisle and sat a couple of rows behind her. "Look, here he comes," said one of them.

"He's gorgeous," said the other. "I sure would love to play Lorna if he gets the part of Jack."

"So would I. He's a hunk. I think his name is Kirk or something like that."

Beth looked up just in time to see the gorgeous hunk they were gushing over. *Kurt Parker. I met him at the sign-up table. They were right. That coal black hair and sexy smile. He's got to be close to six feet tall. I wonder if they noticed the steel gray eyes.*

Beth heard the gasps from behind her when Kurt stopped and spoke to her. "I just wanted to wish you luck, Beth," he said.

"Thank you. Good luck to you too."

"Thanks."

He would make a great leading man, Beth thought as she watched him turn and take a seat in the third row.

Beth jumped in her seat when she felt a tap on her shoulder.

"Sorry. I didn't mean to startle you."

She turned quickly at the sound of Will's voice. "Will. It's you. I'm just a bit nervous. I thought it might be Ted."

"No, but he sent me over to check on you and tell you to look in his direction."

Beth slowly glanced over at Ted. His smile and thumbs up immediately calmed her jittery nerves.

"I thought that might help," said Will.

Beth smiled. "It did. So did seeing you. Thank you for coming over."

Will nodded. "As Casting Director it's my job to touch base with all the actors so you don't have to worry about being seen with me."

"I know and I'm not. It's just that it's been so long since I've done anything like this, Will."

"You'll do just fine. We're about to get started. We'll talk later."

As Will walked away, Beth looked over at Ted one more time. He was still watching her. She gave him a slight nod before turning back to face the stage.

"Ladies and gentlemen! Could I have your attention please?"

The voices stopped and all attention was directed at Mrs. Donaldson who was standing at a podium in front of the orchestra section.

"Please take your seats so we may begin."

Once everyone was seated, Mrs. Donaldson resumed.

"First, on behalf of the Board of Directors of the Tucker's Landing Little Theater and our Casting Director, Will Donaldson, I would like to thank you all for coming here today. I would also like to thank Mr. Ted Lamont, the gentleman who wrote *Mistletoe Madness,* and ask him if he'd come up and say a few words before we begin."

The crowd applauded when he got up and headed for the podium.

Ted stood behind the mic and raised his hands, gesturing for them to stop. "My thanks to Mrs. Donaldson, the Board, Will and to all of you. I'm happy to see such a great turnout for our first day of auditions. As you know, Will Donaldson will be both the Casting Director and the Director." He gestured toward Will who was in the first row.

"The two gentlemen next to him are members of the Board of Directors. Dan Atkins is a retired drama coach who has helped with the production of several other plays at this theater as well as others. My good friend, Jonathan Blake, better known as crime writer, J B Blake is a well-known author with many years of experience as a theater critic. Both Dan and Jonathan, as well as Mrs. Donaldson, will be here to help and offer suggestions. I'll be here to co-direct and help in any way I can, but Will has the final say. I'm confident he'll do a great job."

After a round of applause for Will, Ted continued. "I look forward to working with you and discovering new talent. Good luck to all of you."

Once again, the crowd clapped as Ted stepped away from the podium. He stopped and shook a few hands on the way back to his seat. When he got to Beth, Ted leaned forward, touched her shoulder and whispered "Good luck, Cinderella" in her ear. *I hope no one heard that,* she thought.

Chapter 21

Ted

Ted always sat in the mid-section of a theater during auditions. From this vantage point, he was able to get a good sense of each performer's stage presence. He paid particular attention to body language, how comfortable they appeared on stage and how well the person could project his or her voice. It allowed him to jot down his notations without distracting the person who was on stage. Positioned with one leg crossed over the other and a large notebook propped on his knee, Ted felt comfortable. Being in a theater again, made him feel at home. He couldn't help comparing this small-town community theater to the ones he was used to in New York.

I've worked in smaller ones, he thought. *Many off Broadway with a seating capacity of only one or two hundred. Converted store fronts, old school buildings, some in basements. Unisex dressing rooms and uncomfortable, cramped seating. The smell of hot, buttered popcorn coming from the concessions in a packed lobby.* He smiled at the memories from his days before Broadway. *But I have to say, Tucker's Landing did a great job converting an old movie house into a theater that now seats 400.* He pictured the heavy red curtain going up on opening night. *Almost makes me miss Broadway.*

He silenced his phone, slipped it in his pocket and listened to Will address the group of thirty or more hopefuls who had signed up for the first day of auditions.

"I trust you've all pre-registered online and received copies of certain scenes from the script. We'd like each of

116

you to be familiar with all the roles, not just the one you're auditioning for. You may not get the part you signed up for. However, we might think you're a good fit for a different part or ask you to audition for the role of an understudy. In that case, we'll ask you to read again tomorrow."

Ted scanned the group. His eyes stopped at Beth. *I wish I could sit next to her for moral support, but she's right. It wouldn't look good. If she reads the way she does with me, she'll do fine.*

Will continued, "We have five women trying out for the role of Lorna Hollingsworth and four men for the part of Jack Slater. These are the two leading roles and require a good strong singing voice as well as acting ability. We plan to cast at least six singers who will join the rest of the cast in the office party scene. Are there any questions?"

A young man in the second row raised his hand.

"Yes," said Will.

"When do you think you will announce the cast?"

"Auditions should be over by the end of the week. We'll notify the cast by Tuesday. We'd like to start rehearsals by the end of next week."

Will looked out at the group. "Mrs. Donaldson has given you a schedule of who will be called up to audition this morning. She'll have a schedule for this afternoon after we break for lunch. If there are no more questions, let's get started."

Before returning to his seat in the front row, he turned toward his aunt. "Mrs. Donaldson will call each of you up to the stage. And yes, we are related. Aunt Muriel, you're on."

* * *

Ted shifted in his seat, as Kurt Parker, the third actor to audition for the part of Jack Slater, was called up to the stage. He remembered seeing this one stop to speak to Beth earlier. *I hope he's better than the first two. One of them didn't have a strong enough singing voice. The other didn't seem right for the lead but he's a good possibility for another part. I'll speak to Will about him.*

Ted looked down at the list in front of him. *Good. This is the last one before we break for lunch.* He glanced over at Beth. She was tapping her fingers on the script in her lap. *She's nervous. I wish I could sit next to her. I'll try to talk to her during the break. She probably won't like it, but if she can talk to Will, she can talk to me. I know she wants to.*

He turned his attention back to the young man and watched how he approached the stage. *He fits the image of Jack Slater. Tall. Good looking. He appears confident. Let's see if he can act.*

By the time Kurt Parker was halfway through his audition, Ted knew they found their leading man. He observed the Board members. Dan and Jonathan were smiling and nodding to each other. The minute Kurt began to sing, Ted knew he had Muriel Donaldson's vote, for whatever it was worth. And Ted assumed her suggestions would influence Will a lot. He circled Kurt's name on his list. *Yup. He's Jack Slater. There's only one more trying out for the lead. He'll have to do one hell of a job to top this guy.*

Mrs. Donaldson was beaming, as she stepped back up to the podium. "Thank you, Mr. Parker. That was wonderful. Thanks to all who have already auditioned. We'll take a forty-five-minute lunch break. You have the schedule for this afternoon. We have one more to audition for the role of Jack and two more for the part of Lorna coming up when we resume. Then we will begin auditions for the other roles. Please be back on time."

Ted was about to get up to stretch his legs when Will sat down next to him. "What'd you think of that last one?"

"We still have one more to listen to, but I think we've got our leading man."

"I agree," said Will. "He's fantastic. Muriel thinks so too."

Ted smiled. "I got that impression. He read his lines perfectly and I'm sure he could be heard at the back of the theater."

"Yeah." Will laughed. "No problem there. Muriel sure likes him."

"No question he's a damn good singer," Ted commented. "Dan and Jonathan seemed impressed, as well."

Will nodded in agreement. "I think he'd be good with Beth, too."

Ted made a notation in his notebook. "I'd like to hear the two of them read together."

"Definitely," said Will. "Beth is the second one after the lunch break. I know she's nervous, but once she's on the stage, she'll be fine."

"I'm sure of it too," Ted agreed. "I'll try to talk to her for a few minutes before she goes on."

"Muriel brought sandwiches and cookies for us. They're in the kitchen. I told Beth to have lunch with us so we could discuss set designs."

"Sounds good."

Will started to get up. "See you in the kitchen. Oh, here comes Jonathan now."

"Don't get up," said Jonathan. "We're heading out, but we'll be back. I just wanted to tell both of you we think it's going well. That last one blew us away."

"He seems like the whole package," Ted replied.

Jonathan looked at his friend. "I think the fact that it's a Ted Lamont play is bringing in talent we might not have attracted otherwise. We've never had this big a turnout for auditions before. We can't thank you enough for allowing us to use it."

"Happy to do it, buddy."

"See you after lunch."

When Jonathan walked away, Will got up. "I don't know about you, but I'm ready for lunch."

Ted got up too. "Yeah. It's been a long morning. Let's go grab a sandwich so I can see Beth before she auditions."

Chapter 22

Beth

"Ah, there you are," said Will, as Beth entered the small kitchen. "Ted's over by the table talking to my aunt. Come on, I'll bring you over. He's waiting for you to eat."

"You said we need to talk about set designs."

Will put one finger to his lips and lowered his voice. "That was just an excuse so you could have lunch with us."

Beth started to leave. "I shouldn't be here. How will it look?"

Will took her by the arm and gently pulled her back. "Beth, you really need to stop worrying about how things look. You and I have been friends since we were kids. I don't need a reason to have lunch with you. Besides you're a volunteer."

Beth smiled. "You're right. I overthink everything."

Will shrugged his shoulders. "If it'll make you feel better, I can introduce you to a couple of stagehands."

She laughed, in spite of herself. "You always did know how to make me laugh."

"What's so funny?" asked Ted.

"Speak of the devil," said Will, as Ted approached them. "If I'm interrupting anything..."

Will let go of Beth's arm. "No. Of course not. I was just trying to calm down our little Nervous Nellie."

Ted looked at Beth. "Nervous?" he asked.

"You could say that."

"Listen," said Will. "I have something I need to take care of. Why don't the two of you grab some lunch and I'll join you in a bit."

Ted nodded in agreement. "Sounds good." He took Beth by the hand and headed for the food.

He let go of her when they got to the table. "I don't know about you, but I'm starved," he said. "Everything looks good. What would you like?"

"You go ahead. Don't worry about me."

"You need to eat something," he said. "I don't want you fainting up on that stage."

"I'll have a couple of cookies."

Ted took a turkey sandwich off the platter, put it on a paper plate and added a few chips. "Here, I'll split it with you. You need food, sweetheart."

"Tell that to the butterflies in my stomach."

He held the plate in front of her. "I know you're nervous, but you've got this. You know you do."

To appease Ted, she took one tiny bite of the sandwich. "I don't know why I'm so nervous. You'd think I was trying out for Broadway."

He took the other half of the sandwich. "I'll let you in on a little secret. I've worked with hundreds of actors and actresses over the years, both off and on Broadway. They all get nervous before an audition. Even the professionals."

Beth's eyes opened wide. "Really? Even big stars?"

"They're the worst. They're up against some heavy competition and worried about their careers."

She forced another small bite. "I'd feel better if I could read with you."

Ted chuckled. "Coming from someone who's afraid to be seen even talking to me in the theater."

Beth smiled at her own foolishness. "I know. I know."

His expression turned serious. He stared into her eyes. "Remember, Beth, I gave you encouragement, nothing more. You already had the talent."

To Beth's surprise, she finished her half of the sandwich, some chips and a cookie. "You were right," she said. "I feel better."

"And you'll feel even better once you're on that stage."

* * *

Beth sat back and watched the last actor to audition for the part of Jack. *He's not as handsome as Kurt Parker and he's not as good a singer, but his acting is very good.*

She glanced over at Ted. He was writing something in his notebook. *I wonder which one he liked the best. I wonder what he'll write about me.*

Beth turned her attention back to the young man who was now leaving the stage. *I hope Kurt gets the part.*

Mrs. Donaldson was back at the podium. "That was Drake Dawson. Thank you, Drake. Nice job."

She looked out at the audience. "Next, we have Beth Piedmont. Beth is auditioning for the part of Lorna Hollingsworth."

Beth took one last deep breath, stood up and stepped into the aisle. *How did I let them talk me into this*, she thought, as she moved toward the stage? *What if I open my mouth and nothing comes out? Stop it. No one talked me into anything. I want this part.*

She made her way up the four wooden steps where a stagehand was waiting for her. He gave her the script and quietly slipped back behind the curtain. Beth walked over to the center of the stage and faced the audience. She saw Will in the front row and knew he was silently cheering her on. Ted was sitting further back and apart from the others.

"Whenever you're ready," said Mrs. Donaldson.

When Ted gave her a little nod, it was as if someone had opened a window and let the butterflies out. *You were right,* she thought. *I can do this. I won't let you down.*

She smiled in his direction and began to read.

Chapter 23

Beth

Beth sat across from Ted in what had become one of their favorite spots for a quiet dinner. "I can't believe October's almost over and that we're in the second week of rehearsals," she said. "How do you think it's going?"

"Great," answered Ted. "Will thinks so too. How do you feel about it?"

"I'm not as nervous now. I think the cast is perfect."

He smiled. "I'm particularly fond of the leading lady."

"The leading lady is starving."

Ted signaled to the waiter. "Me too. Let's order."

After ordering their food, Ted handed the menus back to the server. Once he was out of earshot, Ted turned to face Beth.

"Now that our meal is ordered, and we have our wine, why don't you tell me what this big news is that you couldn't tell me about at the theater? The suspense is killing me."

Beth leaned forward and folded her hands on the table. "I'm sorry. I didn't mean to be secretive. I didn't want to talk about it at rehearsal. Too many interruptions there. I wanted us to be alone."

Ted took a drink of his wine. "Good idea. If you won the lottery, it's better that we keep it a secret for now."

Beth's smile vanished. "I'm afraid my news isn't all that exciting. But it's important to me and I wanted to share it with you."

Ted reached for her hand. "I'm sorry, Beth. I was joking. If it's important to you, then it is for me too. I'm listening. No more teasing. I promise."

Her eyes lit up again. "Well...you know that I finished the makeover of Annie's room last week."

"Of course. You did a great job."

She took a deep breath and let it out. "I may have gotten two more customers from it."

"Honey, that's wonderful! Who are they?"

"Ed Farmer's sister has been wanting to redecorate their bedroom for a while. When he showed her Annie's new room, she called and invited me to take a look at it. She loved my ideas and wants to go ahead with it."

"Fantastic. Who's the other one?"

"A woman from Annie's book club wants to talk to me about turning her husband's office into a den now that he's retired."

Ted smiled and picked up his glass. "It sounds to me like you're back in the business of interior design."

"They're small jobs, but that's about all I can handle right now."

He put his glass back down. "You don't give yourself enough credit."

"I couldn't have done it without you, Ted. I owe you so much."

He raised his hand in the air. "You don't owe me a thing. You've come a long way in the past couple of months and you did it on your own. All I did was offer a little encouragement."

"You're right. So much has happened so quickly since I've moved here. I'm working for Val, involved in community theater and starting my own business. Not to mention playing the lead in a Ted Lamont play."

"You deserve a lot of credit. You've accomplished a lot in a short time."

"Maybe I do, but your encouragement played a big part in helping me get my confidence back and rebuilding my self-esteem."

"It was always there, Beth."

"You talked me into thinking I could play Lorna. You believed in me."

"Friends do that for each other. Will encouraged you to work on the sets. He believed in you. So did Val when she gave you a job."

"You made me believe I have talent and got me back on the stage."

"I only recognized it and helped you see it yourself. I didn't give it to you."

She lowered her eyes. "You made me feel things. Things I thought I would never feel again. You've been there for me, Ted."

He reached over and gently stroked her hand. "And I always will be."

* * *

Ted

The waiter served the coffee then quickly slipped away. Beth dropped one sugar into her cup and added cream. The spoon clinked as she stirred. Ted liked that they didn't always have to talk. *It's nice when two people can be comfortable in each other's company without having to fill every minute with conversation,* he thought.

It had been a long day for both of them. Ted was glad Beth wasn't too tired to go to dinner. *Our lives have been hectic these last few weeks. I've been putting in a lot of hours on a new movie and stopping in at rehearsals as often as possible. Beth's been busy with auditions, her new job, decorating Ann's room, set designs and now rehearsals. It hasn't left much alone time for us. We needed a quiet, relaxed evening together. This is perfect.*

Ted took a long sip of coffee and noticed Beth was staring at him. "Is something wrong?" he asked.

She touched the corners of her mouth with her napkin and tilted her head a little. "I was about to ask you the same thing. How come you're so quiet all of a sudden?"

"Oh, just thinking."

"About?"

Ted chuckled. "About how wonderful it is to be able to sit with someone and not have to talk."

She let go of her spoon and rested her hand on the table beside the cup. "I hadn't thought about it like that, but you're right. It is a nice feeling."

"Yes, it is." He reached over and took her hand. "It also says a lot for a relationship when two people can enjoy quiet moments together."

Beth smiled. "I'm so glad you wanted to go out to dinner tonight."

"I thought we could use a few hours away from all the craziness of late."

"You were so right."

"I had another reason."

"Oh? What was that?"

He took a very slow sip of his coffee. "I have a surprise for you."

"A surprise?"

He loved seeing the excitement in her eyes. "I have something I want to ask you."

"Why didn't you ask me before dinner?"

"I wanted to hear your news first."

"You heard it. Now please stop with the theatrics and tell me whatever it is before I burst."

Ted laughed. "Okay. You've heard me mention my friend, Drew Connor."

"Of course. The playwright from New York."

"Yes, well his new play is opening on Broadway just before Thanksgiving."

"That's wonderful. Will you be going to see it?"

He squeezed her hand. "Only if you come with me. Drew will have two tickets for us at the box office on opening night."

Beth's mouth flew open. "Are you serious?"

"I'm very serious."

Still holding onto her hand, Ted leaned forward. He lowered his voice. "Beth, we've come a long way in the past couple of months."

She looked back at him and nodded. "I know."

"I'm hoping you feel comfortable enough with it to go away with me. It would be good to spend a whole night together. I'd love to wake up next to you in the morning."

"I'd like that too."

"Does that mean you'll go with me?"

"Of course, I'll go with you."

"Good. I'll make the hotel reservations in the morning. It'll be during the break from rehearsals."

"What perfect timing."

"We'll have a wonderful time. I'll take you shopping and to lunch in Central Park."

"Sounds wonderful to me. I can't wait."

"I intend to spoil you."

"Be careful. I could get very used to that."

New York City

Chapter 24

Beth

Beth stood by the floor-to-ceiling windows of their elegant suite and watched as big white snowflakes clouded the magnificent view of Central Park.

Ted came out of the bedroom and stood behind her. He wrapped his arms around her waist and looked over her shoulder. "It's picking up a bit."

"Funny," she said. "At home, the snow would be an annoyance. But here, it almost seems magical."

"You won't think it's so magical if it keeps up."

She turned a little to look at him. "You don't think they'll cancel the play, do you?"

He kissed her cheek. "No, sweetheart. This is New York. The show will go on. But they are predicting two to four inches."

"I guess I'd better wear my boots."

"A limo is picking us up for dinner. He'll take us to the theater and the after party and then back here. You won't have to do much walking, but it's probably not a bad idea."

Beth turned and looked up at him. "You're spoiling me."

"Are you having a good time?"

"Are you kidding? Christmas time in New York, a suite overlooking Central Park, shopping on 5th Avenue, a romantic dinner last night and now dinner and a Broadway show. Not to mention being driven around in a limo. I'm having the time of my life."

"Good. So am I."

His smile made her realize she left something out. "Ted. I left out the most important reason I'm having such a great time."

"What's that?"

"Seeing and doing all of this with you. I've been to New York before. But I've never enjoyed it like this. You make everything wonderful and exciting."

He pulled her closer and looked into her eyes. "Beth, I care for you a lot. I think you know that. I've been afraid to tell you just how much. Afraid I'd scare you away."

"Oh, Ted…"

He interrupted her. "Let me finish before I lose my nerve. You're very special to me. I wanted our first trip together to be fun for both of us. I want you to be happy."

Beth smiled and fought back happy tears at the same time. "You're very special to me too. These last few months have been wonderful. You've made me happier than I have ever been. I'm not going anywhere."

"Good. Because there's still tonight and then tomorrow. Weather permitting, we're taking a carriage ride through Central Park and having lunch at Tavern on The Green."

Her eyes widened. "Oh, I'd love that. I hope this snow stops."

"Me too. I want our last day here to be one we'll always remember."

He gave her a quick kiss. "Go finish getting ready, Cinderella. Your coach will be here shortly."

* * *

Ted

Ted hadn't given much thought to the afternoon flurries. The snow added to the holiday atmosphere of the city and

Beth loved it. When she left the room, he checked the weather on his phone again. *Still saying two to four inches.*

He went back to the window. *It's coming down at a good clip. Damn. There goes the carriage ride and my surprise. If we can still do lunch, I'll go to Plan B.*

Beth came back into the room carrying her boots. "I'm ready. Just have to put on my boots. Anything new on the weather?"

"They're still saying two to four. We'll keep an eye on it."

He stopped short when he turned to face her. "You look gorgeous! I can't wait to show you off."

She smiled. "Thank you. I'm nervous about meeting your theater friends."

"Don't be. They're just people."

"Yeah, important people."

He placed his hands on her shoulders. "The only person who's important to me tonight is you."

"I'll get our coats while you put on your boots."

"Are you worried about driving home tomorrow if this gets bad?"

Not wanting her to worry, he brushed it off. "We're from New England. Two inches of snow is nothing to us. Besides, we can always stay an extra night."

Beth stood up and let him help her on with her coat. She wrapped the pretty blue scarf he bought her around her neck.

"That looks nice on you," he said.

"Thank you."

He let his own scarf fall over his shoulders and put his arm out for Beth. "Shall we go, Cinderella?"

Beth laughed. "It's a good thing it didn't snow the night of the ball. Cinderella would have broken her neck running down the stairs in these boots."

Chapter 25

Beth

By the time they left the restaurant, the powdery white flakes had turned into heavy wet snow. Ted adjusted his scarf and took Beth's arm.

"Still think it's magical?" he asked.

She pulled the fur hood over her head. "I'm back to thinking annoyance."

He ushered her into the waiting limo. "Any change in the forecast?" he asked the driver.

"They're predicting four to six inches now, Sir."

"Great," he muttered before getting in next to Beth.

"Did I hear him say four to six inches?" she asked.

He buckled his seatbelt. "Yup. But don't you worry. The theater isn't far from here."

Beth smiled. "Don't **you** worry. This New Englander isn't about to let a little snow ruin a wonderful evening."

Ted put his hand over hers. "Good girl."

She sat back in the seat and looked at his profile in the darkness. *What I am worried about is what your New York friends are going to think when you introduce me. They're used to seeing you with beautiful, younger women and Hollywood actresses, not a nobody who does community theater.*

On the way to the theater, Beth thought about the last time she was in New York City and the Christmas play she went to with her girlfriends. *Ted's name was on the marquee. I had no idea then who he was then.*

She remembered the fun and excitement. *The crowd, the lights, the applause. It made me wish I hadn't given up the theater.*

A few minutes later, the sleek, black limo pulled up in front of the theater. Beth could see the bright, white lights that lit up the marquee through the tinted windows. *Who would have thought I'd be going to the opening of Andrew Connor's new play, They Call Me Alice, with Ted Lamont? In my wildest dreams I never could have imagined being here with this man. Starlets eat your hearts out.*

The driver opened the door. The snow was blowing sideways. Ted helped her out. She had to walk with her head down. Holding his arm, she let him lead the way.

The snow was slushy and slippery. Ted held onto her, so she didn't fall. Once inside, he headed for the box office.

"Ted Lamont! Is that you?" shouted a booming voice through the crowd.

When they turned, a tall dark-haired man who appeared to be about Ted's age was walking toward them.

The man extended his hand to Ted. "I heard you were going to be here tonight."

Ted smiled and shook the man's hand. "Harry. How've you been, old buddy?"

"Not bad."

"Harry, I'd like you to meet Beth Piedmont. Beth, this is Harry Saunders. He's a producer. We go way back."

Harry held out his hand to Beth. "It's a pleasure to meet you."

"Nice to meet you, Mr. Saunders."

"Please, call me Harry. I've known Ted since before his Broadway days."

He looked at Ted. "It's great to see you again. How do you like living in Massachusetts?"

"I love it."

"Same town as J B Blake, I heard."

"We're neighbors."

"That's great."

"It's been good talking to you, Harry, but I have to get to the box office and pick up my tickets. Tell Joyce I said hello."

"I will. She's around here somewhere. Will I see you at the party later?"

"We'll be there."

"Great. We'll catch up there."

Beth took a deep breath as Harry turned and disappeared into the crowd. *That wasn't too bad.* She followed Ted to the box office where he was waited on by an older woman with short blonde hair.

"Good evening, Mr. Lamont. Nice to see you again."

"Good evening, Stella. Good to see you too. You should be holding a couple of tickets for me."

She opened a drawer and pulled out a white envelope. "I have them right here. Great seats, by the way."

He smiled and took the envelope. "Thanks, Stella."

"You're welcome. Enjoy the show."

Ted opened the envelope and showed the tickets to Beth. "Stella was right," he said. "These are great seats."

"Wow. Any closer, we'd be on the stage."

He put the envelope in his inside coat pocket. "Let's mingle a bit before we go in."

For the next twenty minutes, Beth smiled her way through the parade of Ted's theater friends who just had to say hello and tell him how much they missed his plays.

"If it isn't Ted Lamont. Tired of small town living yet?"

"I knew you couldn't stay away long."

"Broadway needs another Ted Lamont play. When are you coming back where you belong?"

The happy look on Ted's face made Beth wonder if he really did miss his old life. She could easily see how much he enjoyed the excitement of the theater on an opening night.

When a bell rang and the lights flashed, Beth knew it meant the show would start soon.

Ted looked at the people standing around them. "I guess we should be getting to our seats. It was great to see all of you."

He took the tickets out of his pocket and put his arm out for Beth. "It's show time, Cinderella."

* * *

Ted

Being in a theater again brought back good memories for Ted. He remembered the flurry of excitement as people scurried around backstage making last minute changes to scenery and props. Actors rehearsing their lines. He laughed to himself. *Arguing with directors, Worrying about reviews. Fear of a flop.*

Ted was grateful to his long-time friend, Drew Connor, for inviting them to tonight's opening. He was looking forward to seeing the successful playwright again. Although they hadn't seen each other since Ted left New York, they kept in frequent touch with one another. *It was good of him to invite us. I can't wait for him to meet Beth.*

Looking down at the leaflet he held in his hands, Ted thought of how Josephine had saved the playbill from one of his earlier plays all these years and how much it still meant to her. It felt good knowing something he created could give people joy. *The theater is different than any other form of entertainment. We get to see how an audience reacts and hear the applause. You know you have a hit. There's nothing like the thrill of an opening night. You don't get that feeling from writing a TV movie. I do miss that part of it.*

Ted looked at Beth. That feeling of anticipation you get before the curtain goes up showed on her face.

"You miss it, don't you?" she asked.

Caught off guard by her question, he shrugged. "Sometimes, I guess."

The lights dimmed before he could say anything else. He covered her hand with his. "Curtain's about to go up."

Chapter 26

Beth

The cold, wet snow had accumulated to well over four inches in the last couple of hours and showed no signs of stopping. The sidewalks were slippery. The theater's maintenance people had shoveled pathways to the curb and put down sand. The streets were a mess, making it difficult for the cars and limousines to pick up their passengers. Horns honked as frustrated limo and taxi drivers fought for the limited spaces.

Ted spotted their driver on the other side of the congested street. "He's over there. We're going to have to make our way across. Hang on to me."

Tiny pieces of ice pelted Beth's face. She nearly fell twice. *Definitely beyond annoyance now. More like treacherous* she thought, as they trudged through the slush.

Once back in the comfort of the limo, she loosened the wet scarf, pushed the hood off and fluffed her hair.

"I can just imagine what this is doing to my hair."

"You look gorgeous."

"Thanks, but I think you may have a biased opinion."

He reached over and squeezed her hand. "Happy?" he asked.

She smiled and faced him. "The happiest I've ever been."

"I promise we won't stay too long at the party. Just long enough to have some champagne and hear a couple of reviews. It's getting late and the roads are slippery."

Beth sat back and tried to relax. *I wouldn't be disappointed if we didn't go at all. I wish he hadn't told everyone I'm playing the lead in one of his plays for community theater.*

These people are professionals. I'm sure they're wondering what he's doing with an amateur.

But it wasn't only that. Beth had a bad feeling about the party. She couldn't put her finger on it, but it nagged at her. *Maybe it's just the storm.*

She glanced over at Ted. *Am I afraid I won't look as good to him now that he's around all these young actresses? Or am I worried that tonight made him realize how much he misses New York and Broadway? He did admit he misses it.*

"Think you'll ever write another play?" she asked.

He hesitated before answering. "I have."

She opened her eyes wide. "I had no idea you were even working on one."

Ted touched her hand gently. "I started it over a year ago. I put it away when I moved and picked it up again a few months ago. I wanted to surprise you when I finish it."

"You don't have to tell me everything you do, Ted."

He reached for her face and gently turned it toward him again. "Beth, I'm a playwright. The theater is in my blood."

Beth forced a smile. "I know."

"That doesn't mean I would up and move back to New York."

"But…"

"I have no intention of giving up my home on the ocean." He kissed her gently. "And certainly not of giving you up."

Chapter 27

Beth

The small function room at the back of the restaurant was packed. "This is what you call a few friends?" asked Beth. "There must be forty people in here."

"Thirty-eight, now that you two are here."

Beth spun around. Ted was shaking hands with a slender, dark-haired man in a tuxedo. He was slightly shorter than Ted and had more gray at the temples.

"Beth, this is Andrew Connor, the man of the hour and our host this evening. Andrew, meet the lovely Beth Piedmont."

He raised both brows, revealing eyes as gray as clouds before a storm. "Ah, the new Lorna. Ted's told me a lot about you. I have to say, he knows how to pick a leading lady."

"I've heard a lot about you too, Mr. Connor. I can't tell you how much I enjoyed your play. I'm sure it will get rave reviews."

"Thank you, Beth. And call me Drew. Everyone does. Ted, get the lady some champagne and something to eat. We'll catch up later."

A waiter walked by carrying a tray of champagne. Ted grabbed two glasses and handed one to Beth. "Well, you heard the man. Are you hungry?"

She took the glass from him. "A little."

"Me too. Let's make our way over to the buffet. But first, a toast."

He held his glass up to hers. "To opening nights."

"Lots of them," she said.

"Come on, let's get a bite."

On the way to the food table, Ted ran into more old friends. Other playwrights, directors, musicians, actors and actresses. Some had been in his plays. Harry and Joyce Saunders were at the buffet.

"Well, Beth, how did you like the play?" asked Joyce.

"I loved it. The whole night has been wonderful."

"Except the weather, of course," added Ted.

"You're a New Englander now, Ted. Surely, a little snow doesn't bother you."

Ted laughed. "I've only been living on the coast since the summer. Haven't had much snow yet."

"Funny that you had to come here for it."

"Real funny."

Beth reached for a plate. "Wait till he gets his first taste of a winter storm on the ocean. Everything looks so good."

"It's not like we don't get blizzards here, you know," said Harry. "Try the scallops wrapped in bacon."

"Harry, I see Chuck Monroe," said Joyce. "Didn't you want to talk to him?"

"Oh, yes. If you'll excuse me, Ted. I need to catch him before he leaves. Talk to you two later."

Ted looked at Beth who was adding a finger sandwich to her plate. "Guess I'll try the scallops."

They stood in a corner trying to eat without dropping their food. "You're pretty good at this," Ted commented.

"I mastered the fine art of mingling when I went to events with Carl. I was left alone a lot. I learned when to be invisible and how to make a quick exit."

"There's just no end to your talents."

By the time they finished eating, the room had thinned out a bit. "The ones who came for the champagne and food don't stay long. They'll read the reviews tomorrow. We'll mingle a little more, hear the first reviews and leave."

She followed him through the crowd. More people. More quick introductions. More champagne.

A pretty, blue-eyed, twenty something blonde batted her false eyelashes at Ted. "So, Ted, is Beth in one of your TV movies?"

Beth was annoyed that the girl spoke to Ted instead of addressing her with a question about what she does for a living. She was even more bothered that Ted answered the girl instead of letting Beth speak for herself.

"No. Beth is the leading lady in a little theater production of one of my plays."

The girl didn't seem impressed. "Is that an off Broadway theater?" she asked.

About as far off as you can get, Beth wanted to say. She wasn't sure if the girl was being facetious or if she was actually that dumb.

The brunette standing next to her nudged the girl. "That's community theater, Marcie. Amateurs. Don't you know anything? Come on. I need more champagne."

Ted shook his head as the girls walked away. "The last thing those two need is more champagne."

Beth rolled her eyes. She turned and saw Drew Connor walking toward them. "Here you are," he said. "I was afraid you left already."

Ted thanked him again for the invitation and assured him they wouldn't go without saying good-bye. "We're waiting for the first reviews and then we'll be heading out."

"I'm so glad you both came. Sorry we couldn't have spent some time together, but you know how it goes."

"Oh, I know. There's a lot to do before an opening. When you get to Boston again, we'll do lunch."

He slapped a hand on Ted's shoulder. "Soon, buddy. Soon."

Drew looked at Beth. "I have business in Boston in December. Maybe I can make it to Tucker's Landing for one of your performances."

Beth was about to tell him how much she liked that idea when a loud, female voice cut through the air like a sharp knife.

"Well, well, well. Look who's back in town."

Beth froze. Ted's smile quickly vanished. The chatter stopped. Heads turned as Diana Lange made her entrance.

Drew spun around and faced the angry redhead.

Ted grabbed his arm. "You said she wasn't invited."

"She wasn't," Drew said, over his shoulder. "I'll take care of this."

Drew put on his best phony smile and faced her. "Nice to see you, Diana. Glad you could make it."

Her words dripped venom. "Like hell you are."

He reached for her glass. "I think you've had enough champagne. Why don't we get you some coffee and something to eat?"

Diana backed away, holding her glass in the air. "Oh, no you don't. I'm not finished."

Ted took a step forward. Drew put his arm out to keep him from moving closer. "Take it easy, Ted."

"She's drunk."

"What's wrong Teddy dear? I thought you'd be happy to see me."

Ted ignored Drew's warning. "Diana, what are you doing here?"

"I came to see you, of course. I told you I'd be here."

"What are you talking about?"

"I left you two messages. You really should return your calls, Teddy.

Ted gritted his teeth. "This isn't the time nor the place."

She laughed at him. "I think it's the perfect place."

He moved toward her again. Drew stopped him. "I said I'll handle it."

Drew turned back to Diana. "What is it you want, Diana?"

She lashed out at him. "I wanted a part in your play. You said I was too old."

"I said you were too old for the lead."

Her speech was becoming slurred.

"And you." She looked at Ted. "The great Ted Lamont. Too busy trying to even the score with your small-town girlfriend's ex-husband to do me one favor. And after all we've meant to each other."

Ted pushed past Drew. He grabbed Diana's arm. "That's enough! You're making a damn fool of yourself."

"Ted! Please! You're not helping the matter."

Drew turned to one of the waiters. "Get Security. And hurry."

Beth moved closer. She stood next to Ted. "Let go of her, Ted. Drew's right."

She looked at Diana. "What about Carl?"

Diana said nothing. She glared at Ted. Beth asked again. "Miss Lange, do you know my ex-husband, Carl Piedmont?"

Diana's tone became even angrier. "No, but your boyfriend does."

Beth turned back to Ted. "How do you know Carl?"

"You mean he hasn't told you?"

Beth's eyes were still on Ted. "Told me what?"

He turned toward Drew. "We need to get her out of here."

"I sent for Security."

Beth didn't let it go. "I want to know what she's talking about, Ted."

"We'll talk about this later."

"I want to know now."

Diana took a drink of champagne. "Tell her, Teddy. Tell her who Cynthia had the affair with eight years ago on Cape Cod."

Beth could barely speak. "Please tell me what I'm thinking isn't true."

Ted avoided a direct answer. "Let's not talk about this here."

She looked at him in disbelief. "You knew this from the beginning and never said anything to me?"

He pleaded with her. "Beth, please...let's just go."

Beth couldn't move. He took her hand. She pulled it away.

Laughing, Diana lifted her glass to take another sip. When Ted tried to get it out of her hand, she hurled the rest of the champagne in his face and let the empty glass drop to the floor. She looked down at the broken glass by her feet and then back at Ted. Her expression became serious.

"You shouldn't have broken your promise, Ted."

Drew stepped in and gently moved her away from the broken glass. He motioned to one of the waiters. "Take care of this, please."

Two security guards made their way through as he tried to disperse the curious guests that had gathered around them.

"Everything's fine. Please go back to enjoying your evening."

Ted pulled out his handkerchief and wiped his face and jacket. He stuffed it back in his pocket and walked toward Diana. "I never made you any promises. I'm sorry, Diana. I tried. I really did."

Drew had one arm around Diana. "I'll have someone take you home.

She straightened her shoulders and took a deep breath. "Thank you, but that won't be necessary. My driver is outside. If you would kindly see me to my car..."

"Of course."

"I'll go with you," said Ted.

He turned toward Beth and placed both hands on her shoulders. "I'll only be a few minutes. Then we'll go back to the hotel and talk."

Beth didn't want to talk. Especially, not to Ted. She needed time to think about what had just happened. *What if Diana is right? Is Ted with me because he's trying to even the score with Carl?*

Her head was throbbing. *I need air. I have to get out of here.*

A half an hour later, when Drew and Ted went back to the party, Beth was gone.

Chapter 28

Ted

Ted was checking his phone when Drew caught up with him again by the bar. "There you are," he said. "The reviews will be online shortly. If you and Beth want to cut out before that, I'll understand."

Ted tried to keep his voice low. He didn't want anyone else to hear him. "She's not here, Drew. I can't find her anywhere. I'm worried."

Drew moved closer and lowered his voice too. "What do you mean she's not here? She has to be. Where could she have gone?"

"I've been around the room twice. No one's seen her. She's not answering my text messages."

"Maybe she hasn't checked them. Have you tried calling her?"

"She's not answering her phone either. I left a voicemail."

Drew quickly scanned the room with his eyes. "Well, she can't have gone far. I'm sure she hasn't left the restaurant. I'll check the bar near the dining room. You go to see if her coat's still in the coat room."

Ted turned and nearly bumped into Joyce Saunders. "Ted, what are you still doing here? I thought you left."

"Joyce! I can't find Beth. Have you seen her?"

"I saw her about a half hour ago. She said she was leaving. I assumed with you."

He shook his head, as the fear inside of him grew stronger. "No. She didn't leave with me."

Drew looked at Joyce. "Then she must still be here. We were about to try the bar and the coat check."

"Don't bother with the coat check," said Joyce. "She had her coat on when I saw her."

Ted turned toward Drew. "I don't like what I'm thinking."

Drew put his hand on Ted's shoulder. "Let's not jump to conclusions. Joyce, would you mind checking the ladies' room. Maybe she's in there."

"Sure. I'll be right back."

"OK. Ted and I will check the bar and meet you back here."

Ted followed Drew to the bar in the main dining area. When they saw Beth wasn't there, they headed back to wait for Joyce.

Ted checked his phone again. *No messages.* He rubbed his forehead. "This is all my fault."

Drew sighed. "Not entirely. The dragon lady had a bone to pick with me too. Your being here made for a more dramatic entrance to her little performance. I take it you didn't come through with something you promised her."

"That's the way Diana sees it. She wanted me to get her a part in a TV movie."

Drew shook his head. "So that was the favor?"

Ted nodded. "I told her I'd make a few calls. I swear I never made her any promises."

Drew tapped him on the shoulder. "I'm sure you didn't. Here comes Joyce. She's alone."

"Sorry, Ted. She wasn't in there. I take it she wasn't at the bar either?"

Both men shook their heads.

"I'm sure she's okay," said Joyce.

Drew agreed. "Maybe she decided not to wait for you and took a cab back to the hotel."

Ted turned toward them. "Thank you both for your help. Drew, you've got another hit on your hands. You need to get back to your guests and I need to find Beth.

"Good luck, old buddy. Text me when you find her."

"I will."

Joyce gave him a hug. "Diana tried to come between Harry and me once, but we didn't let her. Don't you let her ruin what you have with Beth."

Ted kissed her cheek. "Thank you, Joyce. I'll try not to."

He hurried to the waiting limo, got in, pulled out his phone and hit Beth's number again. *I'll never forgive myself if anything has happened to her. Please answer.*

Chapter 29

Beth

Beth heard the tires spinning as the cab pulled away from the curb. The driver honked his horn and swore at the car in front of him, who apparently, wasn't moving fast enough. "Don't worry, Miss," he yelled over his shoulder. "All the trains have been delayed. I'll get you to Penn Station in plenty of time."

Wondering how anyone drives in this city, Beth turned toward the window and watched the hotel fade into the stormy night. *I hope I didn't make a terrible mistake.*

She took her phone out of her purse, sat back in the seat and thought about calling Ann. *I need to let someone know I'm coming home earlier than expected and that I'll be alone. How am I going to explain all this to my family? Gram will be so disappointed.*

Beth stared at the blank screen for several minutes while she thought about what to do. *I can't wake Annie at this time of night. It will scare her half to death. I can't call Dylan. He'll just rant and rave. I don't need that right now.*

She shook her head. Between the dispatcher's voice, static and the steady thumping of the windshield wipers, Beth couldn't think straight. *I can't call from here. I'll have to do it from the station. It'll be quieter. At least I hope so. I'll call Val. She's good at handling difficult situations. She can tell Dylan in the morning. She knows how to handle him too. The two of them can tell Annie and Gram together. Yes. That's what I'll do. I'll call Val from Penn Station.*

Once she had that figured out, Beth slipped her phone back in her purse and stared out the window. She thought about Ted. *I wonder if he's found my note yet, or even realizes I'm gone. According to my messages, he hasn't called since he was leaving the party.*

* * *

When Beth arrived at Penn Station, she checked the schedule and took a seat in an area that wasn't too crowded. *The driver was right. I have plenty of time to make my call.* She pulled out her phone and hit Val's number. *I hate to wake her, but I have to let her know in case Ted calls her. And I need someone to talk to.*

"You're where?" asked Val, in a sleepy voice. "Penn Station! What are you doing there? Where's Ted?"

"He must be at the hotel by now."

"The hotel. Why aren't you with him?"

Beth's voice was shaky. "Oh, Val, I'm sorry to wake you but I need to talk to someone."

"It's okay, Beth. Are you all right?"

"Yes. I'm on my way home. I can't go into all of it right now, but I need you to tell Dylan."

"Tell Dylan what?"

"Tell me what?" asked a groggy Dylan. "Who's at Penn Station?"

Ugh. I should have realized they'd be together.

"Your sister. Quiet. I'm trying to find out."

"My sister. Let me talk to her." Dylan grabbed the phone from Val.

"Beth, are you okay? Why are you at the train station? Where's Ted?"

"We had an argument. He's at the hotel. I should be in Boston around 9."

"I'll pick you up."

153

"Dylan, there's no need. I'll take a cab or Uber."

"He let you roam around New York in the middle of the night. What's wrong with that guy?"

"I'll explain that after I get home. Would it be okay if I come to your house instead of going straight to Gram's? I don't want to upset her before she's had her breakfast."

"Of course, you can come here, and you can explain in the car. I'm picking you up. Here's Val. Give her the information."

"Dylan..."

"No argument, Beth. You're my sister. I love you. Don't worry about Gram for now. I'll give Annie a heads up. Talk to Val."

"I love you too, Dylan."

Val fished a pen and a piece of paper out of the nightstand drawer and wrote down what Beth told her. "Okay, sweetie. Text me from the train if you can. We love you and we're here for you."

"I love you too, Val."

Beth hung up the phone and let the tears escape.

Chapter 30

Ted

There were no lights on when Ted entered their suite shortly after 1 a.m. He thought Beth had gone to bed. *That's probably why she hasn't answered my messages.*

He hung his wet coat over a chair, walked across the plush carpet to the bedroom and quietly opened the door. The heavy drapes were still open. There was just enough light coming through the sheers for him to see she wasn't in the bed. He flipped on the light and quickly scanned the room. The bed had been turned down, but not slept in. The bathroom door was open. A bad feeling came over him.

"Beth. Beth, where are you, honey?"

When she didn't answer, he went back to the living room and turned on a lamp. The shopping bags from Saks were on the table. "Her things are still here," he said out loud. "Where the hell is she?"

A thought hit him as he headed back to the bedroom. *Maybe she lost her key or had some kind of problem? I'll check with the front desk.*

He stopped short halfway across the room when he saw the white hotel envelope propped against the lamp on the nightstand. A long velvet box was next to it. He picked up the envelope, sat down on the edge of the bed and read the note.

Ted,

Your deception hurt me more than I can express. Even if you didn't know about Carl from the beginning, hiding it was the same as a lie. You destroyed my trust. Telling Diana was unforgivable.

By the time you get this, I will be on my way home. Sorry I didn't let you know sooner so you wouldn't worry, but I left my phone back in the room. It's just as well. You would have tried to stop me, and I just want to go home.

I left your gifts. I couldn't keep them under the circumstances.

Have a safe trip home.

Beth

Ted let the note slip out of his hands and fall to the floor. He bent forward, put his elbows on his knees and his head in his hands. "Oh God, what have I done?"

He picked up the velvet box and looked inside. The red stones on the bracelet sparkled under the lamp light. *She was so excited when I bought it for her. I wonder how she would have reacted to the other velvet box I had for her. I'll never know now.*

Ted snapped the box shut and dropped it on the bed. *Damn my stupidity! None of this would have happened if I had only told her the truth about Carl and Cynthia that night when I figured it out.*

He thought about calling or texting her but thought better of it. *I should let her cool down a little. Hell, I need a drink.*

He took off his jacket and tie, went into the living room and poured himself a brandy. Sitting on the sofa, Ted took a generous sip of his drink. *I knew she was upset, but to leave like that and not even take the limo.*

Staring at the shopping bags she left behind, he took a minute to let the slow burn of the alcohol calm his nerves. *I can't blame her for being angry after Diana's announcement. Damn Diana!*

He took another slow sip of the brandy then shook his head. *No. This is my fault. I left Beth standing alone and practically ordered her to wait there while I went with Drew to help Diana. It's all because I kept the truth from her. I told myself she was better off not knowing. Where did I get off making that decision?*

Ted took one more swallow and slammed the glass down on the coffee table. *Who was I kidding? I was afraid she'd think I knew all along. Afraid I'd lose her, and I may have anyway. I brought this on myself. Now she wants nothing to do with me and she's out there alone at night on account of me. I have to try to stop her.*

He grabbed his phone and pulled up her number. It surprised him when she answered.

"Beth. Are you all right? I've been frantic."

"I'm okay. Didn't you get my note?"

"Yes. Where are you, sweetheart? I'll come get you."

"I'm on my way home."

"Are you at the airport?"

"No."

She must be taking the train. "Are you at Penn Station? I can be there in less than a half hour. Don't get on the train."

"Ted, please."

"It's dangerous. I don't want you alone. Let me come for you."

"That's not for you to decide."

"Come back. Please. We'll talk. We'll have breakfast in the morning and go home together."

"I can't, Ted. I just can't. Get some sleep. You have a long drive ahead of you. Maybe we'll talk at home. But not now. I need time. If only you hadn't told Diana."

"But I didn't tell her."

"How else could she have known such a thing?"

"I have no idea, but I intend to find out."

"Ted, I have to go. My train is about to leave."

"Text me from the train later, so I'll know you're safe?"

"You'll be sleeping."

"I don't care. Wake me up."

"Good night, Ted."

"Good night, Cinderella," he whispered, after she had already hung up.

Ted thought about going after her. He looked at the almost empty glass on the table. *Probably not a good idea. She'll be gone by the time I get there. I should try to get some sleep.*

On his way to the bedroom, he poured himself a little more brandy. *What the hell? It'll help me sleep.*

After changing into his pajamas, he sat up in bed with the remote in one hand and his drink in the other. He flipped channels, finished his second nightcap and fell asleep.

A few hours later, Ted woke up with a dry mouth and a pounding headache. The room was dark except for the light coming from the TV. The remote was on the pillow next to him. He clicked off the TV, went into the bathroom, took two aspirins and crawled back under the covers.

Chapter 31

Beth

Beth hurried along the platform, dragging her suitcase through the wet, slushy snow the best she could. Icy pellets pecked at her cheeks. She had to keep her head down, making it difficult to see. *I didn't think this through very well,* she thought, as she trudged past the first car, missing the door. *Good thing I brought boots with me.*

She heard a voice calling to her. "Over here Ma'am."

When Beth looked up, she saw a tall, slender young man at the opening of the next car. He waved his arm in the air. "Over here Ma'am. There's plenty of room."

When she got closer, he reached for her arm to help her board. "There you go. Watch your step."

Beth held his arm as he took her suitcase. "I'll put this with the other luggage."

"Thank you," said Beth. "Thank you."

"You're welcome, Ma'am. Take a seat. We'll be leaving shortly."

* * *

Once she was safely on the train, Beth was glad she hadn't given in to Ted and let him come after her. *It wouldn't have helped matters. I'm too angry to deal with him now.* She pulled off her wet scarf, unbuttoned her coat and took out the eticket the concierge had printed for her. Minutes later, an announcement about their departure echoed through the car. A loud whistle blew. Beth felt the wheels rolling, as the train pulled out of Penn Station, leaving the city and Ted behind.

The conductor was the nice young man who helped her board. When he got to Beth, he scanned her ticket. "Make yourself comfortable, Ma'am. It's a long ride, but it's not snowing in Boston."

She could see his face better now. His boyish smile and soft blue eyes reminded Beth of her son. "That's good news," she answered.

Beth leaned back in the seat and turned toward the window. Big flakes of wet snow hit the glass, making long, watery trails that clouded her vision. She watched the tall buildings and landmarks disappear into the night, as the train picked up speed. Beth began to wonder about the way she handled the events of the last twelve hours. *What was I thinking? Leaving like that in the middle of the night? I never even thought about how dangerous it is for a woman traveling alone in New York City. Ted did have a good point. At least there were a lot of stranded holiday travelers waiting for delayed trains. I hate to think what it would have been like otherwise. Maybe I should have waited for Ted and given him a chance to explain.*

She shook her head. *No. What explanation could he have for deceiving me that way? He had to have known from the beginning. He lied to me and maybe even used me to get back at Carl. No matter what he says, I still think he told Diana.*

Beth took a deep breath and stared at her reflection in the window. She needed sleep, but thoughts of Ted wouldn't allow it. Even when she closed her eyes, images floated through her head. Ted, wiping champagne off his face. The pieces of broken glass on the floor. Drew and the security guards. She saw the anger in Ted's dark eyes and felt her own anger when he wouldn't answer her questions. Diana's evil voice still rang in her ears. *How did it all go so wrong, so fast? We were having a wonderful time before that wretched, vindictive woman showed up. Sightseeing, Times Square, shopping on 5th Avenue.* She smiled remembering the outfit Ted bought her and the beautiful red cashmere sweater. *He said it looked like the one Lorna wore to the Christmas party. And the garnet bracelet. I told him it was too expensive and that he didn't have to buy me things. He said it matched the sweater and bought it anyway.*

Could Diana have made it all up to hurt Ted? No. Where would she have gotten an idea like that if he hadn't told her? Besides, Ted would have told me right away if none of it was true, but he avoided answering me. He told her he was sorry. He apologized to a person who had just made a fool of him in public! Then he escorted her to her car with Drew and left me standing there in front of all those people. I was hurt and humiliated. All I knew was that I had to get as far away from Ted Lamont as I could.

The rocking motion of the train lulled her into a restless sleep for the next hour or more. When she awoke, more horrible memories flashed into her mind. Ted trying to stop Diana. Drew trying to hold Ted back. *And me watching Ted walk out with one arm around the woman he claimed he was never in love with. I was shaking and my head began to ache. I couldn't just stand there and wait until he decided to talk about it. I had to get out of there.*

Beth wasn't sure why she didn't take the limo back to the hotel. *I guess I was afraid the driver would call Ted. He didn't see me get into the taxi, but I saw him. He was too busy helping that shrew to notice me.*

Her thoughts drifted back to when she returned to their empty suite. Finding her phone on the counter, she unplugged it and tossed the charger into her purse. *I didn't want to forget it again.*

She remembered noticing the spots of champagne on her dress as she folded it and dropped it into her suitcase. *How can such a beautiful, talented woman have such an ugly streak? And what does a man like Ted Lamont want with her? What is this hold she has on him?*

Beth stacked the gifts he bought her on the table. All except the bracelet. She quickly packed her suitcase and a small tote bag. Using hotel stationary, she wrote a short note to Ted and left it on the nightstand with the bracelet.

Thinking about the bracelet now made Beth rub her bare wrist. *I shouldn't have let him buy me such lavish gifts. I couldn't keep them now.* Beth sighed. *I couldn't have carried the bags anyway.*

Beth wanted to call Val but didn't want to wake her again. She pulled out her phone and scrolled through pictures of her and Ted. Seeing the battery was low, she plugged it into a charging spot. *I wonder what he had planned for today. He seemed so disappointed about having to cancel the carriage ride. I was looking forward to lunch in Central Park. I'll wait until I get home to text him. He'd be sleeping now anyway, which is what I should be doing.*

Feeling a little hungry, she dug a package of crackers and a water out of her tote bag. She also pulled out a magazine she bought at the train station and dropped it on the seat next to her.

When she finished the crackers, Beth looked at her watch. *Still a long way to go.* She slipped the bottle back into her bag and picked up the magazine. *Maybe a little reading will help me fall asleep.*

Halfway into the first article, Beth could barely keep her eyes open. She put the book down, stretched out her arms and yawned. She wrapped her coat around herself, leaned back and closed her eyes. *I think that did the trick. I hope so. I need some sleep before it's time to face my family. I have a very long day ahead of me.*

Chapter 32

Beth

Dylan kissed Beth on the cheek, opened the door and helped her get into his Escalade. He grabbed the handle of her suitcase. "I'll toss this in the trunk. You can tell me why that maniac let you roam around New York City in the middle of the night on the way home."

Beth dropped her tote bag and purse on the floor by her feet and buckled her seatbelt. When Dylan got in, he slammed the door, buckled up and turned off the radio.

Before he pulled out into the line of traffic, she leaned over and touched his arm. "You didn't have to pick me up. I could have taken an Uber."

Looking at his sideview mirror he mumbled, "That's what brothers are for."

She gave his arm a squeeze and took her hand away. "Thank you. I appreciate it."

He turned so she could see his face. "I wanted to do it. I had to see for myself that you got home safely."

She was grateful he had to keep his eyes on the road as he pulled away from the curb so he couldn't see the tears in hers.

* * *

Dylan

Dylan and Beth had been close growing up. Like typical siblings, they had their childish battles, but they always watched out for each other. When Beth started dating, Dylan thought it was his job to look out for her. Since Beth was the oldest, she didn't appreciate interference from an overprotective little brother. She got enough of that from their father.

How many times had he heard her say? "Stay out of my business, Dylan. I can take care of myself."

And she could too, he thought. *Until she met Carl.*

Dylan didn't like Carl Piedmont. He thought his sister deserved better. But since their father encouraged the relationship because Carl owned his own business and would be a good provider, he accepted him. *As long as she was happy.*

Dylan gave her a quick glance. *I stayed out of that and look what happened. He put an end to her career, cheated on her and crushed her dreams.* He hated seeing what that marriage and then the divorce had done to his sister. *She lost a lot of herself when she was with Carl. She was at an all-time low when she came to Tucker's Landing. Then, little by little, she regained her self-esteem. She started working for Val, got back into interior design, volunteered at the Community Theater and now she's on the stage again. I didn't like Ted Lamont at first. Not him personally, but I didn't think he was right for Beth. I was convinced he's in love with her until this. I wish she'd tell me what happened.*

They rode in silence for the first couple of miles. Dylan wished women were as easy to read as the blueprints and specs he was used to dealing with in his business as an architect. He could deal with strict specifications, deadlines, permits and building inspectors. But women were a mystery he knew he would never fully understand. *Life would be so much easier if women came with blueprints.*

* * *

165

Beth

Beth pulled out her phone and checked her messages. *Nothing new from Ted. I guess I should text him and let him know I made it home safely. I better do it now before Dylan starts drilling me about what happened with Ted.*

In her brief message, Beth asked Ted not to call her grandmother's house as she was at Dylan's. She told him Josephine didn't know yet that he would not be spending Thanksgiving with them. She waited for his response.

"Tell me you're not texting him," said Dylan.

"I told him I'd let him know when I got home."

"You're not home yet."

"I don't want him calling the house looking for me. Gram doesn't know I'm home yet. Oh, Dylan, how can I tell her?"

He kept his eyes on the road when he spoke. "Val went over to talk to Annie. Annie will tell her."

Beth took a deep breath and let it out. "As grateful as I am about that, I feel like a coward having Val do my dirty work."

"It's okay. She wants to help."

At that, the tears started again. She took out a tissue. "She's so sweet."

"Beth, you're not alone. We want to help. Whatever it is, you can tell me."

She dabbed at her eyes and blew her nose. "I don't know where to start."

"Why not start by telling me what the argument was about?"

She checked her phone. No response from Ted. "Okay."

Beth told him how they were having a wonderful time until the party after the play. "Then she showed up."

Dylan shot her a look. "Who showed up?"

"Diana."

"He took you to a party that Diana Lange was at?"

"She was uninvited and drunk."

They were close to home when Dylan pulled over and parked the car near the beginning of White Stone Beach.

"What are you doing?"

"I want to hear all of this before we get home. And I don't think I should be driving."

Afraid of how he might react, she understood. "Probably not."

Beth opened her window to let in some air and took a few deep breaths before she continued. She told him the things Diana said and how embarrassing it was for Ted and for Drew and how Drew tried to intervene.

"They should have called the cops and had her ass hauled out of there."

"I think they were trying to avoid that. It wasn't the kind of publicity Drew wanted for his opening night."

She told him what Diana said about Carl and Cynthia and how Ted didn't deny it."

"That's crazy."

"She said he knew from the beginning and was using me to get even with Carl for being with his wife."

Dylan ran his fingers through his hair and shook his head. "I just don't believe it."

"He told me later that he hadn't told her, but how could she have known?"

"He wouldn't answer me. Said we'd talk later. What was I supposed to think?"

"I guess I can't blame you for jumping to the obvious conclusion, but Beth, honey, you should have at least given the guy a chance to explain."

"Dylan, he left me standing there while they walked her out to her car. What was I supposed to do? All I could think of was getting out of there?"

"So, you left and went back to the hotel. Just like that."

She started to cry again. "He never even knew I was gone."

Beth told him the rest and how the Concierge helped her get a train ticket to Boston. "You know the rest."

Dylan leaned across the seat and gave her a hug. "It's okay, Beth. Don't cry. As much as I'd like to punch his lights out for not stopping you from traveling alone like that, I think things will be okay once you two talk this out."

"He wanted to come after me. I told him not to."

Dylan straightened in his seat and wrapped his fingers tightly around the steering wheel. "I've never known you to be so stubborn, Beth. You took an awful chance leaving like that."

"I know. I was angry."

Dylan blew out a breath. "I'll talk to him before Thanksgiving. I take it he's on his way home?"

"I guess so, but he's not going to be with us on Thursday."

"What?"

"I put that in the text too."

"Why?"

"You were right not to like him, Dylan. I should never have trusted him."

Dylan hit his fist on the wheel. "I liked him, Beth. I thought he was a nice guy and good neighbor. I just didn't like him for you. Once I saw the two of you together and how happy he made you, I changed my mind."

"Well, first impressions, you know."

"Beth, for what it's worth, I think the guy's in love with you and I'm pretty sure you feel the same way about him."

Beth knew there was no point in denying that she was in love with Ted to her brother. He'd see right through her. But she had doubts about Ted's feelings. Serious doubts.

Dylan started the car. "I think you should call him and straighten this out before it's too late."

She wiped her eyes and checked her phone one more time. "It may already be too late."

Chapter 33

Ted

When Ted woke up again, he was in a fog. The headache was better, but his stomach was upset. He reached for his phone. It was almost nine. *Damn. I wanted to be on the road by eight.* He gave his messages a quick scroll. *So much for texting me from the train. She should be home by now. She could at least let me know she arrived safely.*

Resisting the urge to text Beth, Ted rolled out of bed and headed for the shower. *I need coffee and breakfast.*

* * *

By the time he finished his first cup of coffee, Ted's headache was gone. He read the rave reviews of Drew's play in the morning paper while he ate. *"Another Smash Hit by Drew Connor." "Connor Still on Top." "His Best Play." It's too early. I'll call and congratulate him later.* Just as the server poured more hot coffee into his cup, he heard the sound of a text message and picked up his phone.

Arrived safely. Please don't call Gram's looking for me. I'm at Dylan's. I think it's best that we don't spend Thanksgiving together. Have a safe trip home.

Ted stared at his phone. He read the message again. *She's uninviting me for Thanksgiving? It's the day after tomorrow. What the...*

He started to text her back but decided against it. *What's the point? She won't even let me try to explain. She thinks I used her to get even with Carl. Doesn't believe I didn't tell Diana any of it. She's being totally unreasonable. I don't need this.*

Ted was so angry he couldn't finish his breakfast. His hand shook when he raised his cup to finish the last of his coffee. *So, she doesn't want to spend Thanksgiving with me. Well Cinderella, maybe it's about time your charming prince takes a little vacation. No sense in going home where I'm not wanted. I'm always welcome in this town. I'll stop by some theaters, see a few old friends, have lunch with Drew. Maybe I'll talk to Harry about my new play. Yeah…I think a well-deserved vacation is in order. It'll be great to spend time in some of my old haunts and catch up with people who'll be happy to see me.*

He signed the check, picked up the newspaper and headed for the front desk to make a few adjustments to his reservation. *Maybe New York is where I belong. Oh, yes…and I'll drop in on Ms. Lange. We'll see how she likes being the one caught off guard.*

* * *

Later that morning, Ted moved to a smaller suite. He spent the afternoon making phone calls to old friends and made a reservation for Thanksgiving dinner at the hotel restaurant. On the day before Thanksgiving, he had lunch with Drew.

"I'm sorry about you and Beth," said Drew. "I'm sure you'll be able to straighten things out and get back together once you've both had some time to cool off."

Ted shook his head. "I don't know. At this point, I'm not sure I want to get back together."

"That's your pride talking. Don't let it get in the way of your happiness, old buddy."

"It's not just that."

"Don't give me that. I know you too well."

Ted laughed. "What are you saying? You think I should apologize. Grovel. Beg her to take me back. The woman has trust issues."

"You've got a few issues of your own, pal."

"Thanks for noticing."

"You're too stubborn for your own good. Think of how Beth must have felt when you apologized to a woman who just made you look like a fool. A woman you had a long history with. You're far from blameless in this, you know."

"You get right to the point, don't you?"

"Would you rather I skirt around it, or tell you the truth?"

Ted knew his friend was right. It was his pride and stubbornness that wouldn't allow him to back down. "I know it was my fault. But she hurt me too."

"Does it matter who is more at fault?"

Ted took a drink of his wine. "What do you think I should do?"

"If it were me, I would have begged and a lot sooner."

Ted shook his head and smiled. "You're such a wuss."

Drew stopped cutting his steak and pointed the knife toward Ted. "You should pack your bags and head home and do it now. Make her listen or you'll end up eating turkey alone tomorrow."

Ted thought about that scenario. "Thanks for the suggestion, but I think I need a cooling off period myself."

"So, you're staying in New York?"

Ted nodded. "For a week or so. Not much to go home to. My daughter will be with her mother for the holiday."

"What about the rehearsals back home?"

"They don't need me there. Probably better if I'm not around."

Drew shrugged his shoulders and went back to cutting his meat. "Maybe it'll do you some good to be around the limelight again."

"I've called a few people I haven't seen in a while. I plan to touch base with some old contacts. Harry Saunders wants to read the play I've been working on."

Drew looked up. "You finished it?"

"Enough for Harry to know if he likes it."

He raised his glass to Ted. "Good for you."

"Thanks."

"Any other plans for your visit?"

"No. Just stopping by a few theaters."

"What about Diana?"

Ted wiped his mouth with a napkin. "What about her?"

"Once she gets word you're around, she'll be looking for you."

"After the other night, you'd think she'd be too embarrassed to show her face."

"Not that bitch. It's all over town. She's basking in the publicity."

"Is she now?"

"Oh yeah."

"Well, between you and me, I'm gonna pay that queen of the silver screen a visit. She's got some explaining to do. And I want to catch her off guard."

"Be careful, Ted. You know how she likes to stir up trouble."

Ted downed the last of his wine. "She's stirred her last pot with me."

Chapter 34

Beth

When the meal was over, Beth picked up her plate and started clearing the table. She needed something to do to take her mind off Ted. *Of all the times for Carl to take them to his sister's in Newport,* she thought. *I suppose it's better though. I'm having a tough enough time trying to convince my family I'm okay. The kids would see right through me. At least I didn't have to cook. I wonder where Ted's eating?*

"Just stack the dishes on the counter. I'll put them in the dishwasher after we put the food away," said Val. "You can help me with dessert when Keith and Jessie get here."

Ann got up to help. "Everything was wonderful, Val."

"Thank you, Annie," said Val. "You don't need to do that. Sit down and relax. Let us wait on you for a change."

Josephine smiled. "Have another cup of tea with me, dear. Valerie and Beth can handle the clean-up."

"All right. If you insist."

Ann reached for the teapot, filled their cups and sat down.

Dylan pushed his chair away from the table and gestured to his father and Ed Farmer. "Why don't we go into the living room and relax until then?"

Harvey Granger patted his stomach. "Sounds good, son. Maybe watch a little TV before my grandson gets here. Excellent meal, Valerie."

Margaret Granger knew her husband and her son. "What you really mean is watch more football and fall asleep in front of the TV while the women clean up."

Dylan didn't see Valerie come back in the room. "Come on, Mom. It's tradition. I'd help in the kitchen, but I'm sure Val would tell me I'm just in the way."

"Try it sometime and I'll let you know," she said.

Dylan got up, went over to her and gave her a kiss. "I'm up for the challenge."

"Far be it for me to interfere with tradition. Go on."

"See Mom? What'd I tell you?"

"Don't forget you promised to play the piano for us after dessert."

"There's always a catch. Come on, Dad. You too, Ed."

Ed Farmer looked at Ann. "It's okay, Ed. Go with the men. Josephine and I will have our tea."

The three men walked toward the living room. "Maybe you can coax Beth to join you at the piano and sing for us later, Dylan," suggested Harvey.

Dylan looked in Beth's direction. "That would be nice."

Beth was too surprised by her father's request to answer. She picked up two more plates and followed Valerie into the kitchen. Her mother was right behind her, carrying an almost empty bowl of mashed potatoes. "Would you like me to cover these and put them in the fridge?" she asked.

"Thanks. The foil is on the counter," Val answered.

"Everything was delicious. You did a great job, Valerie. Why don't you relax? Beth and I can clean up?"

"Thank you, Margaret, but you don't have to do that."

"Nonsense. You did the cooking. It's the least I can do. Besides, it will give Beth and I a chance to talk. We don't get to do that often enough, lately."

Beth wondered what her mother was up to. "She's right, Val. You cooked. Let us clean."

"Well since you put it that way. I wouldn't mind sitting for a while. I'll be in the dining room if you need me."

Beth turned off the faucet. "Let's finish clearing the table first."

"I'm right behind you."

"Just stack the dishes on the counter for now. After we get the food put away, we can rinse them and put them in the dishwasher."

Her mother smiled. "That's my Beth. Always so organized.

Beth shuddered. "Married to Carl, I had to be."

Once the table was cleared, mother and daughter chatted casually while wrapping the leftovers.

"You were right, Mom. I wonder which one fell asleep first."

"It was your father."

"How do you know?"

"He's always the first one to drop off. Dylan at least tries to watch football for a while."

Beth scraped what was left of the carrots into a plastic container and covered it. "You know him so well."

"When you're married to a man for fifty-five years, there isn't much you don't know about him."

Beth put the carrots down and picked up another container. "There was so much about Carl I didn't know."

She dumped the remaining green beans into the container, snapped on the lid, then turned to face her mother. "How could I have been so blind and stupid?"

Margaret Granger put down the box of foil wrap and took her daughter's hands. "It hurts me to see one of my children in such emotional pain."

Beth was immediately sorry for her outburst. *The last thing I want to do is upset my mother on Thanksgiving.* "I'm okay, Mom."

"Carl did his best to keep things from you. You're not blind and you're certainly not stupid. You must stop blaming yourself for the divorce. You deserve much better than Carl Piedmont."

"Daddy will probably never forgive me."

"What?"

"He wanted me to marry Carl. I'm sure he's disappointed and blames me for not being able to hang on to him."

"Is that what you think?"

"It's true. You and Daddy thought he was wonderful. Dylan was the only one who didn't think I should marry him."

"Now you wait just a minute. I know you and your father seldom agreed on anything, but you've never been a disappointment to him."

"Never?"

"Never."

"Not even when he found out he had a daughter and not a son to follow in his footsteps?"

Margaret reached up and touched her daughter's face. "The first thing Harvey wanted to know when he found out he was a father was if the baby was healthy, not whether it was a boy or girl."

Beth was surprised by that. "Really? What did he say when he found out you had a girl?"

Her mother laughed and imitated her husband's voice. "It's okay, Margaret. I bought a box of cigars with the pink band to be on the safe side. I'll save the other box for next time."

Beth couldn't help laughing. She put the rest of the vegetables in the fridge while her mother wrapped the turkey in foil. "You never told me that before."

"You never asked."

"I guess I didn't.

Margaret stopped for a minute. "Beth, you need to understand something. Your father grew up in a time when men were the so-called breadwinners. I hate that term, but that's the way it was. He didn't believe in women working."

"But you worked when Dylan and I were little."

"I worked in your father's office because he couldn't afford a bookkeeper. As soon as he made more money, back home I went."

With the food put away, they moved over to the sink. Beth started rinsing the plates. "He never let you work again."

"No. I cooked and cleaned and did the laundry and ran the house. No work for me."

They both laughed.

"He didn't understand why you wanted to be an interior decorator."

"Neither did Carl."

Margaret rolled her eyes. "When you talked about becoming an actress, I thought he'd have a stroke for sure."

"He didn't think I had any talent."

"That wasn't it. He wanted something better for you than that."

"He wanted me to marry Carl. That didn't exactly turn out better."

Margaret handed Beth the glasses. "He's never forgiven himself for taking your dreams of the stage away from you or for not encouraging you to be an interior designer."

"But he's never said a word to me about it."

"Believe me, Beth, your father does not think you couldn't hang on to your husband. He thinks Carl was a bad husband and a poor excuse for a man. When he found out Carl was running around with other women, he wanted to strangle him with his bare hands. Harvey has no tolerance for philanderers. It's Carl he'll never forgive for hurting his daughter."

Beth turned off the faucet and closed the dishwasher. "We should get back out there."

"Beth...wait."

She touched her daughter's arm. "I thought you were upset about your children being with their father today."

"I am."

"This isn't about Carl or the children, is it? It's about Ted."

"Keith and Jessica will be here soon."

Margaret squeezed Beth's hands. "Oh, Beth. I'm so sorry. I hope the two of you can work things out. He's been such a positive influence on you. You've been happier than we've seen you in years."

"I hope so too."

"We're looking forward to seeing you on the stage next month."

"You're both going to the play?"

"Of course. Your father is more excited about this than he's been about anything in ages. He tells everyone his daughter is starring in a Ted Lamont play."

Beth hugged her mother. "Let's go wake up the men before Keith gets here and eats all the pie."

Chapter 35

Ted

Strategically placed fairy lights, crisp white linens and fresh fall flowers on the tables made for a festive atmosphere in the hotel's elegant dining room. The outstanding wait staff catered to its guests as they served an excellent Thanksgiving feast. For the most part, the room was filled with families and couples enjoying a holiday meal. A few lone diners, like Ted, were scattered amongst the mix. It was the loneliest holiday Ted could remember since his divorce. He never realized how lonely a person could be, even in a crowd. *Being surrounded by people isn't the same as actually being with them. I miss being with people on Thanksgiving. Having family and close friends around the table. Eating too much stuffing. Kids fighting over the wishbone.*

Ted sat back and let the waiter remove his empty plate. "Would you care for coffee with your dessert, Sir?"

About to finish his third glass of wine, Ted was ready for coffee. "Yes, please."

"And do you know what you would like for dessert?"

"I'll try the apple pie."

"Good choice, Sir."

Ted sighed. *It won't be as good as Beth's, but I'll make do.*

While he waited for his coffee and dessert, Ted looked around the room. The young couple at the next table were lifting their glasses and toasting something. *An engagement maybe*, Ted wondered. A feeling of emptiness hit him. He thought of Beth and the plans he had for their last day in New York and the carriage ride he had to cancel. *I thought*

I was going to have so much to be thankful for this year. Beth and I would have been celebrating our engagement if things hadn't gone so wrong. Maybe Drew was right. Not sure I know how to grovel though.

Suddenly, Ted had an urge to send Beth a text. He took his phone out of his pocket and held it in his hand for several seconds. *What do I say? Happy Thanksgiving could be taken wrong in a text. What if she thinks I'm being sarcastic? I could call her, but it's not very private here. Besides, she might sense insincerity in my voice. How do you wish a happy holiday to someone who chose not to spend it with you and told you so in a text message?*

When Ted saw the waiter coming with his coffee, he dropped the phone back in his pocket.

After dinner, he went back to his room. *Well, at least I can watch football and fall asleep in front of the TV.*

He picked up the remote, sprawled out on the sofa and let his thoughts drift back to the conversation he had with his daughter earlier. He called her to wish her a happy Thanksgiving and didn't mention being alone or in New York. Ted let her assume he was home. *Holidays are difficult enough when your parents are divorced. No need to add stress to her day by giving her a reason to worry about me.*

"Happy Thanksgiving, Daddy. Say hello to Beth for me."

"Thanks, baby. We'll have lunch soon."

"Okay. Don't eat too much. Enjoy the game."

"I won't."

Ted hung up. He put his phone down and picked up the remote. *I'll try, but it's not much fun watching the game alone.* He sprawled out on the sofa and clicked on the TV.

When he woke up, the room was dark. Ted wasn't sure how long he'd been sleeping, but he didn't know who won the game and he was hungry again. He flipped on a light, turned off the TV and got a water out of the mini-fridge. He sat down at the desk, opened his laptop and pulled up the draft of his new play, *Second Chances*. *If I want this ready to show to Harry Saunders, I better get some work done.* The sound of his stomach growling made him push his laptop aside and reach for the phone on the desk. *But first, a turkey sandwich and a little more of that stuffing. And, what the hell, another slice of pie.* He hit the button for Room Service and shook his head. *I miss rummaging through the fridge and making it myself. Is it still considered leftovers when a chef is making it up special for you?*

While waiting for Room Service, Ted made a fresh pot of coffee. *No more wine tonight. I need to get into work mode.* He changed into sweatpants and a tee shirt, took out his briefcase and turned off the TV. *There. That's more like it.*

Ted worked until two in the morning. He got up at eight, showered, made another pot of coffee and ordered breakfast. He spent most of Friday and Saturday making last minute edits to his manuscript. He had breakfast and lunch in his room and only went downstairs for dinner. When he was satisfied that the play was ready for Harry Saunders to read, Ted closed his laptop. *I'll get a few hard copies made tomorrow so I can drop one off to him on Monday. That's enough work. I'm supposed to be on vacation.*

Chapter 36

Ted

The week started out great. The temperature warmed up and the snow was almost gone. Ted was glad to be past Thanksgiving. He met with Harry and gave him a copy of *Second Chances*.

"You don't know how excited I am to have a Ted Lamont play in my hands again," said Harry.

Ted tried to curb his own excitement. He didn't want to just assume Harry would like it. "Maybe you should save your enthusiasm for after you've read it."

Harry put the manuscript down, leaned forward and opened the wooden box that was on his desk. "If you say so."

He shooed Ted away with the wave of his hand before taking a cigar out of the box. "Joyce and I are going away for a few days. Give me at least a week. I'll be in touch."

Ted smiled, as he got up to leave. "Thanks Harry. I'll wait to hear from you."

The rest of Ted's first week of vacation went well. He stopped by theaters, both on and off Broadway, where his name had once been on the Marquee, caught up with old friends and made sure he was seen by people he might need later. He sat in on a rehearsal and a couple of auditions. Drew found him the address where Diana was staying, but he hadn't had the time to drop in on her yet. *I'll save that for next week.*

Revisiting these places made Ted think about what Drew said. *Do I miss the limelight of working in live theater, or is it just the people I miss?* Ted gave it some thought. *I don't miss dealing with auditions and temperamental actresses or the agony of waiting for reviews. The advantages of what I do now, far outweigh all that. I can work from anywhere. I make my own hours. I love Tucker's Landing and living near the ocean. I see my daughter more often…and then there's Beth. What will I do if Harry wants to produce my new play?*

No matter how busy he was during the day, once Ted was alone in his room at night, his thoughts drifted back to Beth. More than once, he picked up his phone and almost texted her. Each time, he thought better of it. *What would I say? Did you have a nice Thanksgiving? How are rehearsals going? She hasn't tried to contact me either. Better to leave well enough alone.*

Near the end of his second week, Ted ran into Elliott Stone at a party. Elliott was a playwright he knew before his Broadway days.

"It's great to see you, Ted. Is this a visit or have you moved back?"

"Just a visit, Elliott. I'm happy with the work I'm doing."

"You don't look very happy."

Ted hadn't realized it showed. "It's nothing to do with my work."

Elliott gave him a cautious look. "I heard about the incident at Drew's opening night party."

"Drew and I handled it the best we could."

"Don't let it get to you. You, of all people, should know better than to let Diana Lange's theatrics get under your skin."

Ted knew he was right, but that wasn't what was eating at him. He couldn't shake the feeling of loneliness, even in a crowd. *Other people can see I'm unhappy. Why can't I just admit it and do something about it? I should take Drew's advice. Go to Beth and make her listen.*

He left the party and went back to his hotel. Not wanting to sit alone in his room, Ted opted for the bar. The bartender slapped a cocktail napkin down in front of him. "Good evening, Mr. Lamont. What can I get for you tonight?"

"Good evening, Sammy. Jack on the rocks."

Ted pulled out his phone and checked his messages. With his head down, he didn't see her image in the mirror behind the bar. Her voice cut through his thoughts like a sharp knife.

"Hello, Teddy."

He looked up toward the mirror. Without turning around, he spoke to her reflection. "What are you doing here?"

"It's not good to drink alone, Teddy."

His jaw tightened. *So much for catching her off guard,* he thought. "I prefer it."

"You don't mean that. Do you mind if I sit down?"

"Yes, I do mind," he said, still without talking directly to her.

She pulled out the chair next to him and sat down. The bartender placed Ted's drink in front of him and dropped a napkin in front of her. "An Appletini please."

Just what I need. I hope that's her first one. He took a drink of the Jack Daniels and turned toward her. "What, are you stalking me now? Haven't you caused enough trouble? How did you even know I was here?"

"Everyone knows you're back in town. You haven't exactly been hiding."

Ted glared at her. He kept his voice down, but there was no mistaking his anger. "What I do. Where I do it and who I do it with is none of your damn business. You got that?"

"I just wanted to talk to you."

"You could have called."

"You don't answer my calls. Besides I wanted to talk to you in person."

He took another drink. "After what you did, you should know enough to steer clear of me."

"Oh Ted, that's one of the things I want to talk to you about. I want to apologize."

"Apologize! You crash Drew's party, make a spectacle of yourself and a fool out of me in public and now you want to apologize? You never apologized to anyone in your life."

She dabbed at the corner of one eye with a napkin. "Don't be like that, Teddy. I'm sorry about what happened. I mean it. I was angry with you."

"You were angry at me, so you needlessly hurt the woman I want to marry. Now you want me to forgive you. Great performance, Diana. The tears are a nice touch sweetheart, but I don't buy any of it. Save it for the stage…if you're ever on one again."

Her tears stopped as suddenly as they started. "You're going to marry her?"

He looked away and lowered his voice. "Not now. You ruined that too."

"How did I do that?"

He downed the rest of his drink and signaled the bartender for another and then turned to face her again. "I'm glad you're here."

"Why?"

"I was going to come to see you before I leave anyway. I want some answers from you."

She looked nervously around and then back at Ted. "Why don't we go to your room?"

He loved seeing her in the hot seat for a change. "Right here will do just fine."

She took a hefty sip of her drink. "All right. What do you want to know?"

"For openers, how do you know Carl Piedmont."

"I don't."

"Don't lie to me Diana."

"I'm telling you the truth."

"Then how did you find out about him and Cynthia?"

She took another drink, put the glass down slowly and looked at him. "I figured it out."

"What do you mean?"

"I thought it was odd that your new girlfriend had the same last name as the guy your ex was involved with before your divorce. Piedmont."

"I never told you his name."

"We lived together, Teddy. I knew all about that affair and a couple of the other ones she had."

"How?"

She shrugged. "I spent a lot of nights alone when you were working. One night I was looking for something to read and…"

Ted's eyes widened. "You found the detectives report and read it."

"I was bored."

"That stuff was private. It was none of your business."

He turned away from her. "Damn you, Diana!"

"It didn't seem like that big a deal at the time. I knew your ex had affairs. You told me some of it."

"I never thought you'd stoop so low that you'd use it against me. How could you do that? How?"

She put one hand on his. "I'm sorry, Ted. Really, I am. I don't know why I said those things. I had too much to drink. I was angry. I was jealous. You hurt me and I wanted to hurt you back. I didn't intend to hurt Beth in the process. You have to believe that."

"Why did you tell her I was using her to get back at Carl?"

"Because the thought had crossed my mind."

Anger boiled inside him. He pulled his hand away. "You thought I could do something like that?"

She grabbed his arm and forced him to look at her again. "No. I know you better than that."

He wanted to believe her. "I'd like to believe you, but you've burned too many bridges with me."

"Believe me, Ted. This one time, please believe me. I'll apologize to Beth and tell her I made it up, if it will help."

He saw something in her eyes he'd never seen before. *Could it be sincerity? I doubt it.*

"That won't be necessary. I have to get myself out of this. She's angry because she thinks I knew about Carl and Cynthia from the beginning."

"But you did."

"No, I didn't. I didn't connect the name the way you did. She never told me the first name of her ex or what he did for a living. If she had, I would have put it together. It wasn't until she mentioned his name and the name of his company and that he had an affair eight years ago with a woman on Cape Cod that it hit me."

She let go of his arm. "And you didn't say anything."

He stared at the glass in front of him. "No."

"And that's really why she left New York?"

"How did you know that?"

"You're here alone and you're drinking Jack Daniels. I don't need a detective for that."

He shook his head. "Guess not."

She finished her drink and picked up her purse. "I'm sure she'll come to her senses. You're a good man. She knows that."

"Are you leaving?"

"I have an early flight in the morning."

"Oh? Going somewhere?"

"Back to Hollywood. My ex is producing a new movie. He thinks I have a good chance of getting the lead."

Ted wasn't surprised by her announcement. *She always lands on her feet.* "That's nice. I'm happy for you."

I'm also happy she won't be hounding me for that TV part now.

"That's why I wanted to talk to you in person. I couldn't leave with things so bad between us. I wanted to apologize."

Ted thought he detected sincerity in her voice. "Thank you for that, Diana. Good luck in Hollywood."

"Thanks. I hope things work out for you with Beth."

"Yeah. Me too."

She reached over and hugged him. "Good-bye Teddy."

Ted watched her walk out of the bar and out of his life for what he hoped would be the last time. He realized Drew was right. *I can't throw away my happiness because of stubbornness and foolish pride.*

189

He finished his drink, signed the check and headed up to his room to pack.

Chapter 37

Beth

Beth was happy to get back to rehearsals, but nervous about seeing Ted again. They hadn't spoken since he called her at the train station. He didn't respond to the text she sent him two days before Thanksgiving. *I guess I can't blame him. I did uninvite him for Thanksgiving dinner in that text.*

She arrived at the theater almost an hour early. Will's car was the only one in the lot. *Good,* she thought. *Ted's not here yet.*

Beth thought about what she was going to say to Ted when he got there. *I can't very well ask how his Thanksgiving was. Do I start off with an apology and ask where he had dinner, or wait and let him speak first? If he speaks to me at all. Maybe he won't even be here. Ugh. I could kick myself for letting my anger get the best of me. If I'd just handled things differently. I better get inside. I don't need a confrontation in the parking lot.*

When Beth stepped out of the car, she felt the cold air on her cheeks. She pulled her scarf across her face and hurried toward the building. Once inside, she loosened her scarf, unbuttoned her coat and headed for Will's office. The door was open. He was at his desk. He looked up as she was about to knock.

"Beth. I thought I heard someone come in. You're early."

"I was hoping you might have a few minutes to go over a couple of small changes with the set, but if you're busy, it can wait."

Will pushed what he was working on aside. "It's okay. I can finish this later."

"Well, if you're sure."

When he smiled, it reminded her of the boy who used to mow her grandmother's lawn so many years ago. "Take off your coat and have a seat."

Beth hung her coat on the rack in the corner and sat down. "How was your Thanksgiving?" she asked.

"It was nice. I had dinner with my sons and their families. Their mother was there with her husband."

"That must have been hard for you."

"I've made my peace with it. It makes holidays easier for my boys. I'm glad she's happy."

Beth couldn't imagine spending a holiday with Carl and a new wife. "You're a good father, Will."

"I try."

A sadness came over her that must have shown in her eyes. Will picked up on it.

"What about you, Beth. How'd things go at Dylan's?"

She forced a smile. "It was nice. I missed my kids, of course."

"And what about Ted?"

Beth got defensive. "What about him?"

"I'm sorry. If you'd rather not talk about it, I understand."

She hesitated and looked over her shoulder toward the door.

"Don't worry about Ted walking in on us. He's not coming."

"How do you know that?" she asked.

"He called me. He's staying in New York for a while."

"Then you know he wasn't here for Thanksgiving?"

"Yes."

"Did he tell you about our fight?"

"No. He didn't tell me anything. Just that he'd be staying on in New York. I assumed you must have had an argument."

So, he didn't tell you Diana Lange, his old girlfriend, showed up or that I came home alone on the train in the middle of the night?"

Will shook his head and opened his eyes wide. "What are you talking about? He let you come home alone on the train! What in hell is wrong with him?"

"He didn't let me go, Will. By the time he got back to the hotel I was gone."

"I don't understand. Diana Lange, the actress? What does she have to do with all this?"

Beth couldn't hold back the tears. "Oh, Will. She crashed the party. She was drunk. She created a scene and said terrible things about Ted and Carl and Ted's ex-wife. It was humiliating."

"You're not making sense, Beth."

He grabbed a few tissues from a box on his desk. "Here. Dry your eyes and tell me what Ted did when all this happened?"

She wiped her eyes with the tissues. "He left me standing there and went with Drew to help her to her car."

"What about when he came back?"

"I was gone."

"Gone? Wasn't it snowing in New York that night?"

"Yes."

Will got up and closed the door. "I hope he has a good time in New York because I'm gonna strangle him when he comes back."

She stood up to leave. "I didn't mean to burden you with this. It was just as much my fault for leaving. I should have waited."

Will stood in her way. "Don't go, Beth."

He put one arm around her and gave her a hug. "You could never be a burden to me. I care too much about you."

Beth looked up at him and smiled. "You're such a good friend."

"I love you, Beth."

"Will."

"Wait. Let me finish. I love you as a friend, but I'm not afraid to admit I'd like it to be more than that. I always have."

"I love you too, Will."

He let go of her. "Why don't you sit back down and tell me what happened?"

* * *

Will

Will tried to remain calm and unbiased while Beth told him about their argument in New York. When she got to the part about Ted's ex-wife being involved with Carl and that Ted knew it, he could feel his blood pressure rising.

Will slammed his fist on the desk. "Damn him! And damn that no good ex-husband of yours!"

Beth was close to tears again. "When Ted wouldn't answer me, I became furious. Then when he went with Drew and Diana and left me standing there, I just snapped."

Will regained his composure. "It's okay. I get why you left the party. Go on. What did you do after you left?"

By the time Beth got to the end of her story, Will could see that she wasn't thinking clearly, and Ted tried to go after her. *There's still no excuse for him leaving her at the party in the first place.*

"Beth, I can understand how you felt. I don't blame you for being angry, but you shouldn't have gone off on your own like that in the middle of the night. Heaven knows who's hanging around a train station at that time."

"Oh, there were a lot of people around. A lot of trips were canceled because of the snow."

Will hit the side of his head with his hand. "In my book, Ted should have gone after you."

"But I wouldn't let him."

"I know. I know. But that doesn't matter. He should have…"

Beth held up her hand and interrupted him. "I've had a lot of time to think about it, Will. That part really was my fault. I should have waited for him at the hotel and listened to his side of it and gone home the next morning instead of leaving the way I did. That was stupid of me."

"I still think he should have gone after you no matter what."

"I honestly don't know if he knew about Carl and his ex from the beginning or if he figured it out later and just kept it from me."

"Honey, you never gave him a chance to tell you."

"I realize that now."

Will took a minute before he spoke. "You know, Beth, this may sound strange coming from me since I'm a little jealous of Ted, but he's not a bad guy and I think he loves you. I don't believe he would have used you to get back at Carl. It's just not his style."

Beth stood up. "I hope you're right. But I won't know till he comes home."

She turned toward the door and looked back over her shoulder. "If you don't strangle him, that is."

Will got up and hugged her. "Maybe I won't strangle him."

He turned to open the door and gave her a wink. "But a good swift kick in the ass seems in order."

Chapter 38

Will

Will was pleased with the way rehearsals were going. The cast was upbeat and doing a great job. Even Beth seemed more relaxed. All that changed when Ted returned from New York. Although he sat at the back of the theater and kept away from Beth, his presence alone created tension with the cast members, especially the leading lady. Will noticed a certain edginess in her. She even forgot her lines more than once. Ted's constant scrutiny and comments were getting on Will's nerves. He feared it would come to blows, if Ted didn't back off and let him handle things. It finally did.

* * *

Will lifted his baseball cap and ran his fingers through his hair. He blew out a breath, put his cap back on and shouted, "Okay, cut."

Beth turned and looked toward Will. Kurt threw his arms up in the air.

Will raised a hand. "Take a breather and we'll try it again in a few minutes."

Ted left his seat up the back, hurried down the center aisle and sat next to Will in the front row. "What is his problem?" asked Ted, in a voice that echoed its way to the stage.

Will knew the problem that was causing the obvious tension on the set for the past couple of days didn't stem from Kurt. *But what can I do about it? Everything was going fine until Ted came back from New York. How do I tell him he needs to butt out?*

He shook his head. "I'll talk to him."

That didn't seem to satisfy Ted. "He's blown two lines. They've had to try this scene four times and he can't get the kiss right."

"I said, I'll talk to him."

Will got up and headed for the stage. Beth had turned away with her back to both Will and Ted. Kurt was glaring at Ted. By the time Will reached the stage, Kurt was pointing toward the front row.

"Me!" he shouted. "He's the one you should talk to!"

Will put his hand up. "Simmer down, Kurt."

"You're telling me to simmer down? What about him? I'm not the one blowing the lines and you know it, Will."

Ted got up and moved toward the stage. "I know when a line is missed and when a scene isn't right. Are you forgetting who wrote this play?"

The other cast members stepped out of the way and watched.

Will turned toward Ted. "Ted, please. You're not helping matters."

"He's not giving it enough emotion. Jack loves this woman. He's letting Lorna know how he feels. She's not getting that from him."

"Of course, she's not!" yelled Kurt. "How can she, with you watching her and making her all nervous. There's nothing wrong with the way I'm doing that scene."

"I think I know a bit more about the way that scene should be played," bellowed Ted.

Kurt's face turned as red as the berries in the scenery. "Okay, mister big shot, why don't you come up and show us how it's done?"

Ted took two giant steps forward. In one big leap, he was on the stage.

Beth spun around and faced them. "Stop it, both of you. Have you gone mad?"

She turned toward Ted. "It was my fault. I lost my concentration."

She stepped closer to Kurt. "Ted's concerned because this scene can make or break the play."

Kurt lashed out at Beth. "And you don't think I know that? Well then...why don't the two of you show me how it should be done?"

With that, Kurt walked off the stage and took a seat in the first row.

Shocked at Beth's reaction to Ted's behavior, Will wasn't sure what to do. He turned and faced Beth. "You're okay with this?" he asked.

She glared at Ted. "If it'll stop all this nonsense and get this scene over with so we can all go home, yes."

Will threw his hands in the air and shook his head. He turned toward Ted. "The stage is all yours."

Still shaking his head, Will went back to his seat. *I have to have a talk with him after this.*

Ted moved toward Beth. "Do you remember the way we rehearsed it?"

Her eyes met his. "I remember."

He put his arms around Beth and started to kiss her. Beth tried to push him away.

LORNA: "Jack! What are you doing?"

JACK: "It's okay. We're under the mistletoe."

LORNA: "What?"

(She looks up and sees the mistletoe.)

(Jack takes Lorna in his arms and starts to kiss her again.)

Will thought the kiss lasted longer than it should have. There was no mistaking Lorna's reaction this time. *Or was that Beth's reaction?*

JACK: "Merry Christmas, Lorna."

Still holding her, Ted whispered in her ear. "Merry Christmas, Cinderella."

Beth stiffened and broke away from him. He was about to tell her he was sorry, when she turned and hurried off toward backstage.

***

Ted

Ted felt terrible about what he'd done. He jumped down from the stage and went over to Kurt. "I'm sorry for my unprofessional behavior. You've been doing a fine job. I just wanted you to show more emotion."

Kurt stood up and faced him. "I guess we both got a little too emotional."

Ted knew Kurt was referring to the way he kissed Beth. He let the comment go. *If it was a dig, I deserved it.* He held out his hand. "No hard feelings? I promise I'll leave the directing to Will."

Kurt shook Ted's hand. "No hard feelings."

"Good."

Ted started to walk away.

"Mr. Lamont," said Kurt.

"Yes."

"I just want you to know how grateful I am to be playing the lead in a Ted Lamont play. It's truly an honor working with you, Sir."

Ted smiled. "Thank you. I'm looking forward to a great performance."

Before he turned to walk away, Ted saw Will coming toward them. "Are you two still at it? Haven't you caused enough damage for one day?"

"It's all right, Will," said Ted. "I've apologized to Kurt."

Kurt nodded. "Yeah, we're good."

Will put both hands on his hips and glared at both of them. "Well, that's just swell."

He turned toward Ted. "Your little temper tantrum was the worst display of unprofessionalism I've ever seen. It ruined the rehearsal."

"I know, Will. I'm sorry."

"You wasted everyone's time and reduced our leading lady to tears. What the hell is wrong with you?"

Ted started to walk away. "I'll go talk to Beth and apologize."

"No. I talked to her. She's okay now. I don't want her upset again. But you and I need to talk."

Ted stopped. "Okay."

Will looked at Kurt. "Take fifteen minutes. We're gonna try the scene one more time." He looked at Ted. "With no interruptions this time."

Kurt nodded and walked away.

Will turned to Ted. "Let's go to my office, so we can talk in private."

Ted followed him to the little office backstage. Once inside, Will closed the door. Ted spoke first.

"I'm sorry. You're right. There's no excuse for my behavior. I promise you it won't happen again."

Will dropped his clipboard on the desk. "You're damn right it won't."

He took off his cap, scratched the back of his head and sat down. Ted sat across from him. "Is Beth okay? I'll go talk to her."

"She is now. But I'd rather you didn't talk to her."

"I want to apologize."

Will stared across the desk. "For the kiss, or for what happened in New York."

Before Ted could answer, Will continued. "I know about what happened in New York."

"That's between Beth and me. It's none of your business."

"It is when it affects the performance of my leading lady. More importantly, when a woman I've known and loved since we were kids is hurting and confides in me, I make it my business."

Ted thought about what he said. *So, he's in love with Beth. Not that I'm surprised.*

Will took a deep breath. "Look, I'm grateful to you for letting us use your play. We all are. I appreciate the help and guidance you've so generously offered. But you can't allow your personal feelings to get in the way. You know that."

"Neither can you."

"What do you mean?"

"You don't want me to talk to Beth because you're in love with her, not because you're worried about her performance."

"I said I love her, not that I'm in love with her. Not that I couldn't be if she ever gave me the slightest bit of encouragement."

Will looked away for a second and then back at Ted again. "Don't worry. She hasn't."

Ted leaned forward. "Well, I am in love with her."

Will could barely control his temper any longer. "You used her to get even with that slug of an ex-husband of hers."

"That's not true," Ted shouted.

"I suppose you didn't let her take the train home in the middle of the night in a snowstorm either. You call that love?"

Ted sat back in the chair again and lowered his voice. "I didn't let her do that. She was already gone when I got back to the hotel. She wouldn't let me go after her. She's a pretty stubborn lady, in case you didn't know that."

Will softened a bit. "She did tell me you tried to stop her."

"Did she tell you she refused to let me explain any of it to her or listen to me at all and that she uninvited me to Thanksgiving dinner? In a text, no less."

"No. Not about Thanksgiving. Only that you weren't there. Is that why you stayed in New York so long?"

"I thought some distance might help."

Will shifted in his seat. "I can only tell you the rehearsals were going fine until the last couple of days when you showed up again. She blew the lines, not Kurt. They had no problem with that scene until you were sitting in the theater."

"And you think my presence is causing tension on the set?"

"Yes. And Kurt feels it too. That's why he blew up at you."

Ted thought about it. "I only want to apologize to her."

"All I'm asking, Ted, is that you wait until after the play. Let her be for now. She doesn't need any more distractions."

"The last thing I want is to hurt Beth more than I already have. I'll make myself scarce for the next couple of days. On opening night, I'll sit up the back."

"I think that would be best."

"Again, I'm sorry about today. You're doing a great job directing, by the way."

"Thanks. I hope things work out for you and Beth. For what it's worth, I think she's in love with you too."

Ted shook Will's hand and walked out of his office. *If that kiss was any indication, I'd say he's right. If I could just get Beth to realize it.*

Chapter 39

Ted

Ted stood at the back of the theater with Jonathan. "Almost like old times," said Jonathan.

"Yeah, but this time I don't have to worry about your review," Ted answered.

"If memory serves me right, I already wrote one on this play."

Ted nodded. "And a damn good one."

"Something tells me I'd be writing a good one tonight too."

Ted turned to make sure no one was close enough to hear him. "You know, J B, I'm just as nervous about tonight's performance as I was back then."

Jonathan smiled at his friend. "I know. You're nervous for Beth."

"Am I that transparent?" asked Ted.

"I'm afraid so, old buddy. But don't worry. She'll do just fine and I'm sure things will work out between the two of you."

"I don't know about that. I never got to apologize to her for my ridiculous outburst at rehearsal."

Jonathan gave him a surprised look. "You didn't apologize?"

"Will stopped me. He said my presence was causing tension on the set."

"That's crazy," said Jonathan.

"I didn't want to upset her more, so I agreed to make myself scarce for the remainder of the rehearsals."

Jonathan shook his head. "I didn't know that."

Ted continued. "I shouldn't have listened to him."

"No, you shouldn't have."

"I should have ignored him and apologized to her right then and there."

"I'm amazed that you didn't. Will's not a bad guy. But they do go back a long way. He could even be in love with her."

"He claims he isn't," said Ted. "But it wouldn't surprise me."

"Well, it doesn't matter. It's you Beth's in love with."

A warning bell rang. The lights flashed. "Show time, buddy. Let's head down front," said Jonathan.

Ted didn't move. "I have to sit in the back."

Jonathan turned quickly. "What?"

Ted shrugged. "I promised I'd keep a low profile."

"Another one of Will's orders?"

"Not entirely."

Jonathan kept his voice low, but Ted sensed his anger at Will. "Do you realize how bad that will make us look?"

"I'm sorry. I hadn't thought of that."

"Low profile my ass. The Ted Lamont I know would never let anyone tell him where to sit on opening night, or any other night."

Ted couldn't argue that one.

Jonathan turned back toward him. "I have two seats for us down front. Are you coming?"

Ted moved into the aisle. "Right behind you."

* * *

Beth

Beth stepped out of her dressing room for a few minutes to see how the rest of the cast was doing. The whirlwind of excitement backstage was typical of an opening night at the theater. Nervous performers scurried about, in need of last-minute costume adjustments. Stagehands checked props and mics. Technicians worked on sound and lighting. Kurt was huddled in a corner with a female cast member going over lines.

In an attempt to calm the butterflies in her stomach, she took three deep breaths and let them out. She made her way to the curtain and pulled it back enough to take a quick peek at the crowd coming in.

Beth jumped when she heard the voice over her shoulder. "It's a sell-out."

She turned quickly. "Will! Don't sneak up on me like that. I'm nervous enough."

"Sorry. I didn't mean to startle you. He's up the back."

"Who?"

"Ted. That is who you were looking for, isn't it?"

She answered him too quickly. "I was looking to see if my family is here yet."

"They're here."

What's the use? she asked herself. *He knows who I'm looking for.*

She turned toward Will. "I thought maybe he wouldn't come."

"He wouldn't miss your opening night."

"He hasn't been here since he had the argument with Kurt."

Will rubbed his chin. "Beth…about that…"

"There you are!" shouted a stagehand. "They need you in the sound booth."

Will sighed, shook his head and turned to leave. "Sorry, Beth. I gotta go."

What was he about to tell me? Does he know why Ted stopped coming to rehearsals? Did he have something to do with it?

Beth hadn't seen or heard from Ted since he caused all that trouble over the kiss scene at rehearsal. *I wonder why he never apologized to me like he did to Will and Kurt. Could Will have had something to do with that as well?*

With Will gone, Beth quickly opened the curtain just enough to peek out and see Ted and Jonathan taking their seats up front. She smiled, let go of the curtain and headed back to her dressing room.

* * *

Beth

Once back in her dressing room, Beth sat at her vanity table rehearsing her lines and adding touches of blush to her already rosy cheeks. She dropped the makeup brush when a stagehand banged on her door. "You're on in fifteen minutes!" he shouted.

She raised both hands to her chest and took several deep breaths. "There. That's better."

Beth straightened her necklace and smoothed her hair. She grabbed the edge of the table and spoke to her reflection in the mirror. "Show time."

There was a second knock on the door. This one was soft and there was no warning shout. "Beth, it's Kurt."

Happy to hear his voice, she got up and opened the door. "Come in, Kurt."

"I'm sorry. I didn't mean to interrupt anything."

"You didn't."

Kurt walked in with that usual air of confidence she loved about him. "Oh. I thought I heard you talking to someone."

"Just giving myself a pep talk to calm my opening night jitters."

"Well, whatever you said must have worked. You look fantastic."

"Thank you. So do you."

"I thought we could walk out together."

"Great idea. Maybe some of that confidence of yours will rub off on me."

He laughed. "You're kidding right?"

"Not at all."

His expression turned serious. "You've got something more important. You've got courage."

"More like a lot of nerve."

"This is a tough business. You had the courage to follow your dream and return to the stage after a long absence. I admire you for that."

"Thank you, Kurt. Having you for a leading man helped a lot."

"We make a great team. Don't you agree?"

"I do."

He took her hand. "Pep talks are over. Let's go out there and break a leg."

* * *

Ted

Ted sat back and relaxed in his seat next to Jonathan. *J B's right. Ted Lamont doesn't hide at the back of the theater on the opening night of one of his plays even if it's not on*

209

Broadway. I'll deal with Will Donaldson later. Right now, Beth needs to know I'm here. I saw her peeking out from behind the curtain.

The lights went down. A hush fell over the audience. The orchestra started to play. As the red velvet curtain began to rise, Ted's thoughts brought him back to the night he watched this same play open on Broadway. He felt the adrenalin rush, the excitement, the anticipation of waiting for reviews. Only this time, the exhilaration wasn't for himself. It was for Beth, the woman he'd fallen in love with. *To think she was in the audience the night Mistletoe Madness opened in New York. Now she's playing Lorna.*

* * *

Beth

Beth stood in the sidelines waiting for Will to tell her when to go on. She took several deep breaths in an effort to calm her nerves. Kurt was beside her.

"Don't worry," he said. "Once you're out there, you'll forget about being nervous."

Beth rolled her eyes. "As long as I don't forget my lines."

"Trust me. You won't."

Will came up behind them. "Okay, Beth. Go on out and take your place on stage. You'll have three minutes before the music stops and the curtain goes up. Good luck."

Too nervous to answer, she nodded her head, took one more deep breath and walked toward the stage she had helped to design.

The music stopped. The curtain began to rise. Beth felt the butterflies slowly diminish, as Lorna Hollingsworth emerged and stood in the spotlight. *Kurt was right,* she thought. *And so was Ted.*

***

Ted

Ted Lamont was always the consummate professional. But not tonight. Tonight, he had a difficult time being objective. As he watched Beth breathe new life into a character he had created, Ted's personal feelings overpowered his professional ones. Tonight, his heart ruled his thoughts. *She has great stage presence. I knew she was meant for the part of Lorna that night she read the second act with me in my living room.*

Jonathan leaned in and whispered to Ted. "The audience loves them."

And I love her Ted thought. *The hell with objectivity. Sometimes it's nice to just be a spectator.*

Chapter 40

Beth

The deafening applause was a sound Beth knew would remain in her memory bank forever. *I want to remember everything about this incredible night,* she thought, as the cast stepped forward and bowed in unison. *The lights. The music. The single roses strewn across the floor of the stage. Flashes from cameras and cell phones. And the smile on Will's face when he presented me with a lovely bouquet of red roses.*

"That was one hell of a performance."

"Thank you, Will," she said, as he gave her a big hug and a kiss on the cheek.

Kurt took her hand, brought it to his lips and kissed it. "You were great," he said.

"So were you. A standing O!"

Smiling, Beth waived to the audience and blew kisses to her family. Her smile quickly faded when she turned and saw the empty seat next to Jonathan. *Where's Ted,* she wondered?

Kurt leaned in close to her. "I think he went backstage. Keep smiling."

So, Kurt noticed it too. I hope he's right.

When the applause stopped and the audience was seated again, the cast took one last bow. The red velvet curtain dropped slowly to the floor in front of them. The house lights came on. People moved out into the aisles and headed for the doors. Behind the curtain, excited cast members were hugging and slapping high fives. Beth squeezed her way through the crowd and was almost to her dressing room when she noticed Ted walking toward her.

They stood face to face for the first time since that horrible rehearsal. "Beth," he said. "I was afraid I missed you. Congratulations on an outstanding performance."

The few seconds they stood staring at each other seemed like much longer to Beth. She wanted to hug him and tell him how sorry she was for what had happened in New York, but her arms were full of flowers. All she could do was look at him and say, "I owe it all to you."

He shook his head and gently placed his hand on her arm. "No, Beth. You deserve all the credit. I created Lorna. You made her come to life."

Not sure quite what to say to him, she smiled and said, "Thank you."

Ted hesitated for a few seconds before he spoke again. "Beth, I was hoping we could talk. Maybe go…"

Before he could finish his sentence, Beth's two children appeared and threw their arms around her. "Mom! You were great! It was like watching a Broadway show."

Ted let go of her arm and quickly stepped aside.

"Jamie. Tom. You remember my friend, Ted."

"Of course, Mom. We had dinner at his house," said Jamie. "Nice to see you."

Beth looked at her kids. "He wrote Mistletoe Madness. It's been a Broadway show."

"That's awesome," said Tom, as he reached to shake Ted's hand. "It's a great play."

"Thank you. I'm glad you liked it. And you're right. Your mother put on a superb performance."

Tom turned toward his mother. "Annie's getting the car, so Gram won't have to walk far."

"What?" asked Beth.

"Did you forget Grandpa's taking us to the Black Rock?"

"Of course, she didn't forget," said Jamie. "Mom, you need to get dressed. I'll put these roses in some water."

Somehow, with all the excitement, Beth had forgotten her father's offer to take them out after the show. *I can't talk to Ted now. Do I dare to invite him?*

"It's okay, Jamie. I can do it. I'll meet you outside."

"All right," said her daughter. "But don't take too long."

Once her kids were gone, Beth looked back at Ted. "I'm sorry for the interruption. I would like to have that talk later though."

"It's okay. I have to help Will with something."

She watched his smile fade. "You better go change," he said, as he started to turn away.

"But I wanted to…"

"I gotta go. We'll talk in a few days, after the last performance."

"Ted, wait. I want to ask you…"

He turned and walked away before she could finish her sentence. "…to join us," she said to his back as he hurried off.

Beth didn't see Will come through the crowd. "Were you just talking to Ted?" he asked.

"Will. I'm sorry. What did you say?"

"I said, wasn't that Ted you were talking to?"

"Oh, yes. Yes, it was."

"Where'd he run off to? He seemed to be in a hurry."

"He said he had to help you with something."

"Me? Oh…uh…I better see if I can catch up with him. Will you be okay?"

"I'm fine. I need to change. My family is waiting for me."

"Okay."

Will kissed her on the cheek. "Again...you were magnificent."

"Thank you, Will. And thank you for the lovely roses."

* * *

Beth

Thoughts of Ted whirled through Beth's mind as she hurried to her dressing room. *Why did he leave so abruptly? Was he embarrassed in front of my kids? Maybe he changed his mind about wanting to talk. Ugh. The man is so frustrating.*

When she opened the door to her dressing room, Beth was hit with the fragrant scent of roses. "What the...?"

Cautiously, she stepped inside. "Good Heavens. More roses!"

She closed the door, carefully placed Will's flowers on a chair and walked toward the beautiful bouquet of long-stemmed red roses on top of her dressing table. *Who could they be from,* she wondered? Her heart raced as she remembered Ted coming from the direction of her dressing room a few minutes ago.

"They're gorgeous," she whispered. "There must be at least two dozen."

She pulled the card out of the plastic holder and immediately recognized the handwriting. Tears welled in her eyes as she read it.

Brava, Cinderella.

* * *

Ted

Ted attended every performance but made it a point not to go backstage again after opening night. *I shouldn't have asked her if we could talk. I should have congratulated her and left it at that. She doesn't need added pressure from me right now. This isn't the time to hash over what happened in New York. But after the last performance is over...I'll put an end to this nonsense that's been going on between us for once and for all. It's about time I let her know exactly how I feel.*

Chapter 41

Beth

Beth dragged a step ladder to the center of the stage and stood with her back to the empty seats. Placing one foot and then the other on the bottom rung, she reached for the mistletoe, but couldn't quite grab it.

"Need some help with that?"

She turned her head quickly in response to a familiar voice coming from below the stage. "Ted...I didn't hear you come in."

"Sorry, I didn't mean to startle you."

Beth recognized the two shopping bags from Saks he was carrying. "I was expecting Will. He's going to help me dismantle some of the set and put away the props. I wonder what's keeping him."

Ted placed the bags on two seats in the front row, turned and walked up the stairs to the stage. "I saw him outside. He said to tell you he forgot something. He'll be along soon."

"Oh. Well, I can start without him."

Ted moved closer to the ladder so he could face her. "You did a fantastic job on the set."

"Thank you."

Although Ted attended every performance, he only went backstage to congratulate her once, on opening night. That was the last time Beth spoke to him. She wondered if he was ready to have that talk now and why he brought the bags she left at the hotel.

After an awkward silent moment, Beth spoke first. "So, you're here to see Will?"

"No. I came to see you. I stopped by your house. Annie told me you were here."

"Oh."

She started to climb to the second rung.

"Careful," he warned. "Wait, I'll get that for you."

Her foot missed the step. She grabbed both sides of the ladder in an attempt to steady herself.

Within seconds, Ted was behind her. "I've got you."

Ted caught her in his arms as she fell against him. He lifted her off of the ladder and lowered her to the floor.

He held her until she was breathing normally again. "Are you all right?"

"Yes, thank you. You can let go of me now."

Slowly, he took his hands away. "You shouldn't be climbing like that. You could have broken your neck. What if I hadn't been here?"

He's right, of course, but the last thing I need right now is a lecture.

She took a step back and straightened her sweater. "I know. I know. Can we please leave it at it's a good thing you were here and drop it?"

"I'm sorry. I didn't come here to argue with you."

She gave him a curious look. "Why did you come here?"

Ted nodded toward the bags. "To bring you those. I'm sure you left them behind because you couldn't carry them on the train."

Beth hesitated before answering. "You know that's not why I left them."

He was persistent. "Why did you leave them?"

Is he deliberately trying to embarrass me? She thought. "Under the circumstances, I didn't feel right keeping them."

He reached into his pocket. "Not even this?" he asked, dangling the garnet bracelet he bought for her in the air.

Beth gasped. *If he only knew how much I wished I had kept it.*

"Why did you leave the bracelet, Beth? You could have worn it home."

"I...I didn't think it was a good idea to wear expensive jewelry around a train station."

Ted moved closer. Instinctively, she raised her hand. The deep red stones danced in the light as he secured it on her wrist.

Beth thought of how happy she was when he bought it for her in New York. *Could we be that happy again?* She wondered. "Ted...I..."

He kissed her gently on the cheek. "I bought it for you. No matter how things turn out between us, I want you to have it."

Beth looked at her wrist. *If I don't keep it, his feelings will be hurt. It could destroy any chance we have of getting back together.*

She faced him again. "It's beautiful. Thank you."

Ted smiled. "It looks nice on you."

They stood staring at each other for several more awkward seconds. *If he has something else to say, I wish he'd say it before Will gets here.*

As if he read her mind, Ted broke the silence. "I've missed you, Beth."

Her voice came out barely above a whisper. "I've missed you too."

"Now that the play is over, I was hoping we could talk."

She hadn't seen him since opening night when he stopped by her dressing room to congratulate her.

"That's why you came by my dressing room on opening night, isn't it? To talk."

"Yes."

"But we couldn't talk then. You want to talk now."

He rubbed his neck, nervously and continued. "I have no excuses for my behavior, but I'd like to try to explain at least some of it and tell you how sorry I am about what happened in New York."

Beth wanted that too. *But not here where Will is bound to walk in on us.* "I'd love it if we could talk, Ted. There are things I'd like to explain too, but Will should be here any minute."

"He's not coming back for at least an hour."

"What? How do you know that?"

He looked around the stage then back at her. "When I bumped into him outside, I told him I'd stay and help take down the props if he gave us a little time alone together. He said he'd come back in an hour."

"Oh… I thought we could go someplace quiet. Maybe go for a drink and talk. There are a few things I'd like to know."

Ted shrugged his shoulders. "It's pretty quiet here. We've got an hour to kill. Why not ask me whatever it is you want to know now?"

Maybe he's right, she thought. *If I wait, I may lose my nerve. It could be now or never. Looking directly at him, she asked her first question.*

"Why did you stay away from rehearsals?"

He answered with no hesitation. "Will said I made you nervous. I agreed with him."

Beth wasn't surprised to find out Will had something to do with it. "I see," she said. "I guess he was right. Especially

220

after what happened between you and Kurt over the kiss scene."

Ted looked up at the mistletoe. He banged his fist on the ladder. "I'd just as soon not revisit that episode again, if you don't mind."

His sudden outburst threw her. She blinked and took a step back. *Now I've made him angry.*

"Okay," she said.

When he turned to face her again, she was glad to see he was smiling. "I'm sorry. That was childish of me. Is there anything else you want to know?"

She fidgeted with one of her earrings. "There is one thing I've been wondering about."

He took her hand and cupped his around it. "It's all right, Beth. Ask me anything."

Several seconds passed before she spoke. "Why did you stay in New York so long?"

Suddenly, his smile vanished. He let go of her hand. "I was angry when you didn't want to spend Thanksgiving with me."

Picking up on the anger in his voice, she fired back at him. "Could you blame me? Do you have any idea how much you hurt me?"

"Yes. But you hurt me too, Beth."

"I hurt you?"

"It hurt knowing you thought so little of me. That you actually thought I was capable of plotting and using you to get even with your ex?"

Beth had no words. *He's right. I did hurt him.*

He continued. "You didn't trust me. You wouldn't even listen to my side of it."

221

She automatically shot back in defense. "You wouldn't answer me."

"If you had just waited until we got out of there, I would have."

"Maybe I didn't handle the situation well, but I'm not used to public humiliation. And, you lied to me, Ted. You knew about them. Worse than that, you told Diana."

He shook his head. "I didn't know from the beginning. And I didn't tell Diana."

Beth hadn't intended to start an argument. She wanted to believe him. "When did you figure it out?"

He propped his elbow on a step of the ladder and looked away from her. "The night you told me about your house on Cape Cod. You hadn't mentioned Carl's first name before or what he did for a living."

He paused for a few seconds and then went on. "Cynthia had an affair with a married man when she was staying on the Cape eight years ago. The guy's name was Carl. He owned a drapery business."

"But you knew my name was Piedmont. Didn't you connect it?"

He faced her again. "Honestly, no. His last name was mentioned in the detective's report, but that didn't matter much to me at the time. When you said the name of the business, I pieced it together."

"Why didn't you tell me then?"

He walked away from the ladder and took a step toward her. "I tried, Beth. Several times. I didn't want either one of us to be hurt by the past again. It was a painful memory for me too, you know. For eight years, I've done my best to block the whole thing out of my mind."

A sudden flash of guilt hit her. *Am I that self-absorbed that I never considered his feelings?*

"I'm sorry, Ted. I hadn't thought of the pain it brought back for you as well."

"At the time, I threatened to expose Carl and tell his wife. Cynthia didn't care. She'd have called my bluff. She knew I wouldn't hurt an innocent person, but Carl didn't know that."

"But I heard they broke it off when her husband found out."

"They did. But it was because I threatened to divorce her if she didn't end it and come home. Shortly after that, we divorced anyway."

"What about Diana? If you didn't tell her, how did she find out?"

"We lived together a couple of times, remember?"

He shook his head. "Another part of the last eight years of my life I'd like to forget."

"But how did she find out about Carl and Cynthia?"

"She read the detective's report."

"How do you know that?"

"She told me. Blatantly admitted it."

"When?"

Ted nervously rubbed his chin. "In New York. The night before I left to come home."

Beth turned slightly away from him. "So, you were with her in New York."

He moved toward her. "No. I wasn't with her."

She took a step back. "You told me on the phone you intended to find out."

"Yes. And I planned on it. But she beat me to it."

Beth's voice went up an octave. "Diana went to your hotel room?"

"No! We were in the bar."

Beth folded her arms. "The whole time?"

"I swear, Beth. We were in the bar the whole time. Only long enough for one drink."

"What was she doing there?"

"She said she came to apologize and to say good-bye."

"Good-bye?"

"She's going back to Hollywood to audition for a part in a movie her ex has something to do with."

"And she couldn't leave town without seeing you, of course."

"I had it out with her. She told me she read the detective's report and that's how she knew about Carl."

"She went through your personal papers?"

"Seems it was a hobby of hers. Anyway, she pieced it together and used it to cause trouble between you and me."

"And she succeeded. Oh, Ted, I'm sorry I didn't listen to you. I should have trusted you. I was so hurt and confused and, I hate to say it, but jealous too."

"Jealous! Of Diana? Why?"

"She's a beautiful woman, for one thing, even if she is evil. But mostly because you had a history with her. You loved her once."

He moved toward her. "No, Beth. It's true there's a history there. I told you before, I was never in love with Diana Lange and that's the truth. I hope you believe me."

She reached up and touched his face. "I believe you, Ted."

With one step, he wrapped his arms around her waist and pulled her against him. "You're the only woman I want,

Beth. You'd know that if I could have followed through with my plans for our lunch in Central Park."

There he goes again with that carriage ride.

"Oh, Ted. I don't need a carriage ride or lunch in Central Park to know that."

Just as he leaned forward, his phone rang. "Whoever it is can wait," he said.

"Maybe you should check. It might be Will."

Keeping one arm around Beth's waist, he pulled out his phone. "Damn! Could his timing be any worse?"

Beth giggled.

"Yeah, Will. What's up?"

Beth could hear Will's booming voice. "Sorry to interrupt, but my son ran into a problem on a job. I had to come help him out."

"No problem."

"I'm gonna be here a while longer. Would you and Beth mind taking down the props and putting them aside? Leave the heavy stuff. I'll come by tomorrow with my boys and get it all down to the basement."

Ted looked at Beth and shrugged his shoulders. "Sure. We can do that."

"Thanks. Don't forget to lock up when you leave. Beth has the key."

Ted rolled his eyes. "We won't forget. Have a good night."

Ted dropped his phone back into his pocket and slid his arm around Beth. "Now. Where were we?"

She leaned into him and tilted her head up slightly. "We were killing an hour."

Chapter 42

Ted

Beth placed her hands against Ted's chest, tilted her head back and looked up at him. "Don't you think we should finish boxing this stuff up?"

He tightened his hold on her and kissed her cheek. "No."

She laughed. "No? What do you mean, no? We can't just stand here like this all night."

Her laugh and the sweet scent of her perfume brought back every memory he had of her all at once. He didn't want that feeling interrupted. *I've waited too long to hold her and kiss her again.*

"You feel so good. I just want to hold you in my arms like this and not let go."

"I admit I'm tempted, but what would we say when Will finds us standing center stage tomorrow and the props haven't been put away?"

He leaned down and touched his lips to hers. "This is no time for logic, Cinderella."

She responded without backing away. "Whatever you say."

"I say we pack this stuff up for Will and go get a quick bite."

"Now who's being logical?"

He gently nipped at her lower lip. "One more kiss first."

"I am kinda hungry."

He pulled her closer. "How 'bout we grab a pizza and go to my place? We could finish our conversation over that drink you wanted."

"Sounds good to me. Especially the part about one more kiss."

* * *

Beth

Ted packed office supplies and curtains from the set into boxes while Beth took the ornaments off the tree.

"I'm glad you're here," said Beth. "We'll be done in no time."

"When you're done with the ornaments, I'll get the tree apart and into the box."

"Okay."

"I'm sorry I wasn't here to help you assemble some of the set."

"You probably needed the time away. Did you get together with any of your theater friends or at least have dinner with Drew?"

"I spent some time visiting with old friends in some theaters on Broadway and I had lunch with Drew the day before Thanksgiving."

"I like Drew. Harry and Joyce are nice too."

Ted didn't answer. He walked over and stood by the tree.

Beth smiled. "I'll be done here in a few minutes."

"Beth, I need to tell you something."

She didn't like the hesitation in his voice. "What is it?"

"I went to see Harry at his office while I was there."

"Oh?"

"It was about business."

"I don't understand."

"I worked on Second Chances while I was there. Enough to show it to Harry."

Beth wasn't sure what he was trying to tell her, but her face lit up when she heard he had finished his play.

"You finished it? Ted, that's wonderful!"

She put the last decoration down and hugged him. "Congratulations."

"Thank you."

He pulled away enough so that he could see her face. "Beth, Harry wants to produce it."

Beth had to struggle to keep the smile on her face as the realization of what he was saying hit her. *I was afraid of what might happen when he got a taste of Broadway and the theater again. This must be what he really came here to tell me.*

"Well, of course he does. Why wouldn't he? A Ted Lamont play on Broadway again. You must be thrilled."

"That's the thing. I'm not as excited as I thought I'd be. In fact, I'm not sure how I feel about it."

Beth was confused. "But you're a playwright. You said yourself, the theater is in your blood. Haven't you missed the theater?"

"Not as much as I missed you when I was in New York."

Her smile returned with a few happy tears. "But wouldn't you have to live in New York? What did you tell Harry?"

"I'm supposed to be thinking about it. It would mean spending time in New York, but not necessarily living there. I like living here. Most importantly, I had to straighten things out with you first. I have to know that you're with me no matter what I decide."

He brushed a tear from her cheek with his thumb. "Are you with me, Cinderella?"

Beth looked up at him. *I swear he can see into my soul with those eyes.* "I'm with you."

He gave her one more hug. "I'll pack up this tree and we're done here. Will and his sons can put it all in the basement tomorrow and we can go get that pizza."

She laughed and headed backstage. "I'll get my things."

* * *

Ted

When Beth came back, Ted was looking out at the empty seats. He was thinking about the ring he had in his pocket. *I can't just give it to her over a pizza at my house. She deserves a more romantic marriage proposal than that.*

Beth walked over and stood beside him. "What are you thinking about?" she asked.

He turned toward her. "If you listen, you can hear the applause you got on opening night."

A dreamy look came over her. "I'll never forget it."

"I'm proud of you, Beth. You brought Lorna to life."

"Thank you. Coming from you, that's better than any review. Even if your opinion is a bit jaded."

"That's my professional opinion. Personally, I thought that your opening night performance was the best one I've ever seen, on or off Broadway."

She draped the blue scarf around her neck. "It just occurred to me you left the theater that night before I could thank you for the lovely roses."

"Your family was waiting. I didn't want to take anything away from your night. You deserved to celebrate with your family."

"I wanted you in the celebration too."

He was both surprised and happy to hear her say that. "You did?"

"Of course, I did. I tried to invite you, but you left before I got a chance."

"You did?"

"Yes, I did. You're the person I wanted to celebrate with the most."

"Really?"

"Yes, really. None of it would have been possible without you."

Ted raised his hand and gently stroked her face. "I love you, Beth."

She covered his hand with hers. "It's the first time you've said that to me."

"I've wanted to tell you for a long time. Not knowing how you felt about me, I was afraid I'd scare you away. I was going to tell you that day in Central Park."

She squeezed his hand. "So that's what the carriage ride was about."

"That's why I was so disappointed. I wanted a romantic setting."

"I love you too. I love that you're such a romantic, but I don't need a carriage ride, or a lavish lunch in Central Park."

She opened her arms and spun halfway around. "What better place to hear those words than right here on the stage?"

When Beth spun around, she noticed a prop they missed. "Oh, darn. We missed something."

"What?"

"We forgot to take down the mistletoe. Can you grab it and just toss it in with the Christmas stuff?"

Ted was mulling over what she said about not needing a lavish setting when it hit him. *What better place indeed? Center stage. Under the mistletoe.*

"Sure," he said.

He walked over to the doorframe and reached up. "Beth, can you come over here a minute please? I want to show you something."

"Ted, I'm starved. Can you just take it down?"

"It'll only take a minute."

Beth put her coat down on the desk and walked over to him. "Okay. What is it?"

"You said you don't need an elaborate setting, right? And there's no better place than on stage for us, right?"

"Yes. But what...?"

He pulled her under the mistletoe. "There was something else I had planned for the carriage ride that had to be postponed."

"Ted, what are you talking about? What do you want to show me?"

"First I want to kiss you under the mistletoe where Jack kissed Lorna."

She tilted her head and put her arms around his neck. "Okay."

Ted gave her a long, slow, passionate kiss, like he did at the rehearsal. "You were right. This is just as romantic as Central Park."

Her voice softened. "No wonder you write such great love scenes. Is that what you wanted to show me?"

He reached into his jacket pocket and pulled out the small, blue velvet box he had wanted to present to her since before the snowstorm ruined his plan. "No. This is."

When he opened it, the brilliant two and a half carat, round solitaire sparkled between them.

Beth's eyes widened. Her mouth flew open. Her hands shook as she grabbed his arms to steady herself. "Ted! Oh my God! I don't know what to say!"

"I was aiming for yes."

He looked up at the mistletoe and back down at her. "I want to spend the rest of my life with you. Beth, will you marry me?"

She stopped staring at the ring and faced him again. "You were planning to propose to me in Central Park."

He nodded. "That was my original plan."

"And you came here today to do that?"

"No. I came to make things good between us again. I was trying to come up with a new plan when you were backstage. I was thinking a quiet, candlelit dinner."

Beth laughed. "I love how you always have to set the scene."

He brushed a strand of her hair behind her ear. "I know I'm not very spontaneous, but I thought you deserved a more romantic proposal than that. Then you said there wasn't a more perfect place than on stage."

"I did say that."

He shrugged. "So, I went out of character and did something spontaneous. Instead of moonlight and roses, you got center stage and mistletoe."

She clapped her hands together. "It was the most romantic scene you've ever come up with."

"It's missing one line."

"Oh? What's that?"

"Your answer. Say you'll marry me, Cinderella, so I can put this box away and hold you."

Beth brought both hands up to her temples. "I can't believe it. I forgot the most important line I've ever had."

She wrapped her arms around his waist and moved closer to him. "Yes, Ted. I'll marry you."

* * *

Her hand was still shaking when he slid the ring on her finger. "It's beautiful, Ted."

"I'm glad you like it."

"I love it."

He slipped the velvet box back into his pocket, wrapped his arms around her and pulled her close to him. "Beth, I want you to know I won't make you give up your work or the theater. I'm happy in Tucker's Landing."

"Thank you for saying that. And I'll support whatever you decide to do about Second Chances. I can't wait to read it."

"Other than Harry, you'll be the first to read it. I think we should lock up and get out of here now."

Beth got her coat from the desk. "Would you mind if we stopped by and told Gram and Annie before we get our pizza?"

"Of course not. But forget the pizza. Let's go to the Black Rock for a nice dinner and champagne. In fact, call Dylan and Val and see if they want to join us."

"Okay. We should call our kids from the car."

Ted reached up and pulled down the mistletoe. "I think we can bring the curtain down on this one, Cinderella."

Beth looped her arm through his. "Oh no, my charming prince. This is the second act for both of us. The curtain is just about to go up."

The End

About the Author

Lina Rehal is the author of four contemporary romance novels, two novellas and a book of nostalgia. *Act II* is her latest novel and the third book of her *Tucker's Landing Series*.

Lina resides on the North Shore of Massachusetts. She lives close to the beach and has a lovely view of the Boston skyline. She enjoys Disneyworld, trips to nearby casinos, painting, Karaoke and going dancing with her friends.

She is a member of Red Rock Rewriters, North Coastal Writers, Maine Romance Writers, The Independent Author Network and ReachArts. Lina is on Facebook, X, LinkedIn and Instagram.

She loves hearing from readers and other writers. You may contact Lina through her websites or via email.

Contact Lina Rehal

Email: rehalcute@aol.com or lrehal@me.com

Websites
www.linarehal.com
www.thefuzzypinkmuse.com